Numb

JEFF MENAPACE

2014

For Ma

For everything

THE BAR

I enter the bar—a dive—just before closing. I need to get drunk.

The place is empty save for a bartender wiping down the counter with his back to me. He calls over his shoulder: "Already did last call. Sorry about—"

He turns and my face cuts him off. I place a hundred dollar bill on the bar and slide it towards him.

"That's yours if you lock the door and get me drunk," I say.

The bartender looks at the hundred, then back at me. He's about sixty, heavy, salt and pepper hair.

"You alright, man?" he asks.

I pull another hundred and place it on the bar. "Door locked; me drunk. Yes or no?"

The guy takes the two bills, ducks out from behind the bar, locks the front door, draws the shades, then ducks back under the bar to face me.

"What'll you have?" he asks.

"One glass and one bottle of Jim Beam."

"Ice?"

"No."

He gets the bottle and glass and sets them in front of me. "What happened to you, man? You look really busted-up."

"Thank you."

"Is…is your ear…?"

"Gone? Yes."

"Jesus." He fills the glass with Beam and sets the bottle next to it.

I finish the drink in three gulps. He fills my glass again.

I take a sip and say, "Why don't you grab a glass?"

He shows me his palms. "No thanks—gotta clean-up after."

I place another hundred on the bar. "Have a drink with me."

He doesn't take the bill immediately. "You sure you're alright, man? There's not going to be any trouble is there?"

I chuckle, and my whole body aches. I then finish my second Beam, pour myself a third, and say, "No sir—no trouble. Just offering you a drink."

He slides the third bill off the bar, stuffs it quickly into his pocket as though we've just completed some kind of drug deal, then pours himself a small Beam with ice.

"Cheers," I say, raising my glass.

He clinks my glass and takes a modest sip.

The whiskey is beginning to warm my belly, fuzz my head, and I'm on the verge of entering the *Fuck It* stage.

So I finish my third, pour a healthy fourth, pull the curtain and greet the audience with a bow on the infinitely trodden boards of *Fuck It* , and then start talking to this poor guy as though he wants me to.

PART ONE

KNIGHT IN SHINING ARMOR

1

PHILADELPHIA SUBURBS

I arrived at work and immediately checked my client list.

No.

No.

Yes. She was my last one.

Sound desperate? I'm not. But when you rub naked bodies for a living, you occasionally pine for a star amongst the usual cast of extras.

And Angela Thorne was a supernova.

Let me reiterate; I am not some creepy massage therapist aching to touch beautiful women. In fact, to prove my point, I wouldn't be so eager to massage Angela if she hadn't been the one to start the ball rolling some six months ago.

During those six months of sessions, it had been innocent flirting with an erotic quip peppered in here and there. Harmless stuff, but *good* stuff—an hour that can often feel like a week never went so fast.

Now, Angela was not the first client to ever make a pass at me. Massage can be a sensual art; if you're in the field long enough, it's only a matter of time before the more brazen clientele test their chances, some of them damn fine. And yet, I always respectfully declined. Why? I don't know. Maybe it's that whole thing about the fantasy being better, never giving real life a chance to do its real-life thing and mar that fantasy.

Or maybe I needed a few drinks first.

With a few (or preferably, many) drinks in me, anything was possible. I will openly admit that for some time alcohol has steered my twenty-nine-year-old life and given me the necessary lifts that no antidepressant could ever match. But alas, those lifts were always fleeting. Fleeting, and habitually accompanied by the inevitable drop below rock-bottom come morning.

Come morning when flashbacks of the previous night's debauchery eventually came together and burned my face with shameful recall.

Come morning when the poison thumped my head, leaked nausea from my pores, and frequently jammed an invisible finger down my throat.

Come morning when the depression I didn't think capable of getting worse somehow managed to plummet further still.

But did that stop me from doing it again?

As soon as the hangover and memories of a deeper blue faded, that siren song in a bottle that forecasted zero chance of inhibition would seduce me all over again. *And so what?* I would defiantly proclaim to the only ear willing, no, *wanting* to listen (the *only ear* carrying a prophetic weight I would regrettably come to know). *So what?* It made me feel wonderful, if only for a short, deceitful time, and it stopped all the goddamn voices in my head.

Wait. That's not right.

When I say voices, I'm not talking Son of Sam shit, like I'm receiving homicidal advice from a dog. I'm talking about thoughts. A continuous loop of negativity, reminding me who I am, and what I am. Thoughts of inadequacy and self-loathing that bring my depression further south.

The paradox is that I've been told I give off an admirable appearance to others. I'm no stud or anything (especially not looking the way I do now), but I'm tall, reasonably fit, and on my less-miserable days I would say an above-average face stares back at me in the mirror.

I'm also a good bull-shitter. Not a con-man or anything like that, just able to convince people that my head is filled with optimism as opposed to razor shards from half-empty glasses.

The problem is that it's hard to be "on" all the time. Being a little blue periodically is one thing, but being riddled with feelings of inadequacy 24/7 while your shell tries to portray a different story to the public without cracking? It takes a toll on you. And what does that toll end up costing?

Numbness. You become numb. Act the part long enough, and soon you forget who you are. How to feel.

And that was me. Numb. Numb and…disturbed? Is disturbed the right word? How to explain. Okay, here's a start: I don't like people. In fact, with the exception of a rare few, I must confess an actual disgust for the human race, and, more often than not, I have morbid and violent thoughts playing over and over in my head…

THE BAR

The bartender sets down his drink and takes a step back. I smile what must be a gruesome smile and assure him all is well. He doesn't look assured. I sigh and dig for another hundred, lay it on the bar. He eyes it like it's some kind of rare artifact. I remind him I said the word "was"—I *was* numb and disturbed. I then promise him I'm not anymore (at least not numb—disturbed, no question).

He eventually takes the money, again quick and cautious like it's a drug deal.

I smile the gruesome smile again, notice his drink is near empty, pick up the bottle, and gesture a refill towards his glass. He accepts.

I tell him again that all is well and that I've had enough trouble for a zillion lifetimes, so he needn't worry. As my story progresses he will no doubt grow cagier; the content of my tale will become so sensationally fucked-up and absurd that he will figure me for a drunk (probably, I am) who is embellishing events in his pickled mind (unfortunately, I won't be), or just flat-out lying (again, unfortunately, I won't be).

But this is a good thing. I don't want this guy freaking out halfway through and calling the police or pulling a shotgun out from beneath the bar. If he thinks I'm full of shit and eventually starts to accommodate me with a *whatever you say, pal* smirk as I babble on, so much the better.

Soon he is sipping his new Beam with ice.

I continue…

1 (STILL)

So…how is all my personal bullshit relevant to massaging this woman tonight, you ask? Well, believe it or not, it was all my personal bullshit that got her noticing me from the start.

Crazy, huh? Thinking I'm fooling the world (and for the most part, I believe I was), letting them think that I was as stable as a horse's home, yet after only six sessions with this woman she's able to see right through my act, inform me that my dark side was no secret to her, that I needn't suppress it in her company; she found it intriguing.

It was this uncanny insight and an ability to embrace the unknown from a relative unknown that had me separating Angela from every other offer I'd received in the past. There had to be something or someone out there other than alcohol capable of ripping off my numb-fitted wetsuit (or at *least* tear the fucker), and I thought Angela Thorne might be the one to accommodate me. Her beauty was irrelevant. What lay *behind* that beauty was the real prize. The thing that tickled something inside me I thought all but extinct.

The fleeting, piercing looks I'd catch her indulging in, as if she too had had her share of the exterior and now longed for more essence. The things she would say, their delivery, never actually crossing the line, but taunting it, giving me just enough to fill in the tantalizing blanks on my own.

And believe me I did.

I just wondered, if the time ever came, if I'd have the balls to act on it; or would I end up turning a grand prize like Angela into another one of my consolation fantasies.

2

"Calvin, your four o'clock is here."

She'd managed to sneak up on me in the break room while I was in mid-gulp of a Dr. Pepper. Admirable task for a woman her size. I choked the gulp down, bubbles prickling my nose and eyes. "Thanks, Margaret. She's new right?"

"Yes."

"She filling out a waiver?"

A flash of contempt crinkled the corner of her mouth. "Of course."

I swallowed her attitude and mumbled a thank you. She left.

I tossed the can of Dr. Pepper and headed towards my massage room for final touches. I lit some fragrant candles, dimmed the lights, and switched on the stereo system. Soft music with gentle sounds of nature soon floated from speakers above.

Good to go.

I closed the door behind me, put on a friendly face, and headed up front to greet my new client.

* * *

The session with the new client went well. Nothing noteworthy—a fifty-something woman who was redeeming a gift certificate given to her at Christmas. She was quiet the entire time, even seemed a little on edge. Not all that uncommon; they *are* here to relax. Or it could be that I'm a male. Sometimes the front desk forgets to mention I'm a guy when a client books over the phone, and some women can be understandably uncomfortable being touched by a man they don't know, professional or not.

Guys are always the most amusing—incapable of hiding their apprehension when I first approach, the majority. It's always a good laugh to get them on my table and wait for the first words out of their mouths to be both a test about my heterosexuality, and a rock-solid-goddamn confirmation of *their* heterosexuality:

"The girls in this place are hot, man; you must lov e working here…"

Or something to that effect.

To which I routinely agree, but never without biting my tongue at the thought of casually telling them I was gay. I still might do that one day.

The new client was followed by a regular of mine—a sweet woman who's been my client for over four years now. A pleasure to work with and always tips no less than twenty dollars, bless her.

But enough about all that. Only one client remained tonight…

* * *

"Calvin," Margaret said. She caught me by surprise in the break room again. No Dr. Pepper casualty this time; I was shamelessly checking my reflection in the mirror in preparation.

I turned and faced her.

"Angela cancelled."

Fuck.

I pulled a face of indifference over the disappointed one and hoped it didn't look as transparent as it felt. "Oh yeah? She say why?"

She shrugged. "Nope—just said she wouldn't be able to make it in."

"Oh…okay." I forced a smile. "I guess I can still make happy hour then, yeah?"

She actually smiled back—though hers appeared even more prosthetic than mine—and then headed back up front.

I didn't know what to make of this. Clients cancel all the time, and sometimes, when I'm absolutely exhausted, it's a blessing. Why did I feel as though I was obligated to an explanation as to why Angela cancelled?

If I were to be completely honest with myself, chances were that nothing would have happened tonight in our session that hadn't happened already. It all came down to ego-stroking I guess. I was looking forward to an ego-stroke in my otherwise stroke-less life (take that comment as you will).

Yeah…I guess that made sense.

Dammit, no it didn't. I wanted to see her. Touch her. *Smell* her.

Fuck.

Time for happy hour.

3

The bartender, a cute little blonde, leaned in to take my order.

"Can I have a Jim Beam and a lager?"

"Rocks with the Beam?"

"No, neat please."

She smiled and went to work on my drinks.

Fuck ice, man. I needed the process expedited, thank you. People were crowding next to me, and it was making me nuts. I entertained visions of smashing a beer bottle against the bar and ramming it into the face of anyone studying me, judging me.

I secretly envied all these people I loathed. Is that possible? To hate someone you envy? All these people were *happy* to be here; enjoying every moment to its fullest. I did not see frustration and despair on their faces. I saw contentment and a joy for life. Were they faking it like I was? There was a good chance that a lot of them were drunk, and we are all content and joyous when we are drunk. But what if they weren't? What if they were just happy to be *who* they were and *where* they were?

The bartender set my whiskey and beer in front of me, and not a moment too soon. "Eleven dollars."

I handed her a twenty and told her to keep the change, ensuring future compensation. She smiled back and even winked. I'd like to think it was a pass, but she was likely doing what I'd just done—ensuring future compensation.

Without pause, I began taking my medicine. No doubt after a few more rounds I would gradually build the nerve to mingle with some people, maybe even chat with a woman or two. That was the effect alcohol had on me: it was liquid hypocrisy. My cynical demeanor would blissfully melt away the more inebriated I became. It injected me with a feeling I wished I could bottle and consume every day without fear of hangover or deeper depression.

And trust me, that last one is huge.

Hangovers are one thing; they go away with aspirin, Gatorade, and greasy food. But what many people fail to grasp is that alcohol is a depressant; it brings you up, but boy does it also bring you down. And when you hate who you are, those feelings of inhibition that are so joyous the night before come back at you like a punch in the gut the next day for fear that you might have unknowingly let someone into your pathetic little world.

And yet for some reason, I was willing to swap a temporary high for those inevitable depths of depression, and I hadn't the slightest fucking clue why. It was the American way I suppose. The get-rich-quick way, as opposed to the long, arduous route.

Oh well—fuck it. Cheers.

* * *

I was about four drinks deep when I felt my mood starting to lift. I began to feel a bit surer of myself and immediately ordered another round to make damn certain the feeling would continue. This would no doubt guarantee a more intense hangover the following day, but my booze-laden senses usually skipped class the day they taught foreshadowing (probably sleeping it off somewhere). I was living for the moment (a foreign practice for me sober), and all worries and responsibilities were going to be buried for the next few hours.

* * *

I was probably on my sixth round when I began to think about Angela. My reasoning for drinking tonight (and you *always* needed reasoning) was to ignore any current hazards in my head, and she happened to be one of them. Sure, not the most extreme of reasons, but nevertheless her cancellation this evening did cause me some disappointment that forgave a little drowning.

I found myself staring off into space, replaying the highlights of previous sessions over in my head. Her image was clear and strong. Very clear and strong. So clear and strong it was in front of me.

Literally.

Angela was standing outside; I could see her through one of the bar windows.

I shook my head to be sure what I saw was genuine.

It was her. She was there. But she wasn't alone.

The window was small and did not reveal a lot, but from what I could make out, she seemed to be in a heated argument with someone.

I hurried off my stool and approached the window. I saw a look of fear on Angela's face as a man approached her in an increasing state of agitation.

Was this her husband maybe? Boyfriend? No. She was single—or so she told me. But that could have easily been a lie.

The situation grew more intense as the silent movie I watched elicited body language that told me a physical encounter was a good probability.

The alcohol in my blood forced me to act without consideration. I headed outside.

* * *

The three of us stood in a triangle pattern, a few feet from one another. Both Angela and the man said nothing, just locked their eyes on me, seemingly unsure what to make of my arrival.

I decided to speak first. "Hey, Angela. Everything okay?"

The guy answered for her. "She's fine, man. Fuck off."

His response rattled me. No shouting, no uncontrollable anger. Confident and assured.

"Whoa—come on, man, relax," I said.

He inched closer to me.

We stood about two feet apart, eyes stuck on one another. I had about two inches on him in height, but I would guess we weighed about the same. A good deal of his weight looked like muscle. He had a goatee and a shaved head. And while this particular look can be intimidating, it is a look often sported as a deterrent by pussies who can't really fight. Problem was this guy also sported a crooked nose and scars running through both eyebrows. This told me he'd not only lost his violence-virginity some time ago, but there was a good chance he'd since become a slut.

"Don't tell me to relax, bitch," he said.

Fair enough.

I was tempted to look over at Angela to gauge her reaction to the whole situation, but was worried if I took my eyes off this guy he would crack me one.

I decided to address her directly, all the time maintaining eye contact with dickhead. "Angela, is everything okay? Do you know this guy?"

She finally spoke. "No. I was trying to drop a package off in the overnight slot." She motioned over towards the FedEx rectangle fixed about ten yards from the bar. "He just started bothering me."

Well there ya go. The guy was a complete stranger who was bothering *my* Angela. This was the kind of knight-in-shining-armor shit you saw in movies.

Dickhead smirked at me. "So maybe I was. The fuck are you gonna do, faggot?"

I refused to engage him in a bunch of macho bullshit before the inevitable punch was thrown. It's a fucking fight; not a debate.

He inched closer. We were almost nose to nose.

He who draws first…

I slammed my forehead into his face. Heard and felt his nose crunch on impact. He staggered back, face pissing blood, trying to figure out what the hell just happened.

I didn't give him a chance. I rushed forward. He sensed me coming and covered up, preventing me from landing any decent shots at his jaw and putting him to sleep. I resorted to using my leg like a giant baseball bat, sweeping his legs out from under him. He hit the pavement hard. I immediately punted his head. *BOOM* —goodnight.

If it had been the movie, I would have stopped there. Gone and hugged the girl. But this was no movie; my rage was off its leash. I began stomping his head repeatedly, determined to flatten it like something out of a cartoon.

It wasn't until my third or fourth stomp that a scream from a female onlooker pierced my red haze and stopped me cold. For all I knew this woman was screaming the whole time; I couldn't hear a fucking thing except for my own heart pounding my ears like war drums. Initially, I expected the scream's owner to be Angela, but it was not. She was gone and replaced with a woman I'd never seen before.

I whipped my head in all directions, wide-eyed, the spitting image of a disoriented lunatic I imagine. I desperately wanted to know where Angela had gone, but my urge to exit the barbaric scene I'd just caused finally surfaced and overrode all confusion. I ran to my car and was on the road in less than a minute.

I had no business driving with the combination of alcohol and adrenaline possessing my body, but the thought of stopping the car so soon after fleeing seemed absurd.

I would instead drive a few miles further, and then tuck my car away into a safe spot so I could gather my thoughts, stop my hands and legs from shaking, and talk my stomach out of showing me the whiskey and beer again.

4

A remote shopping center up ahead seemed as good a spot as any to stop. It was after eleven and the center's lot was relatively deserted, a few empty cars scattered here and there. To play it safe, I pulled to the rear of the lot, alongside one of the corner buildings and far away from those scattered cars. Last thing I wanted was a curious cop shining his flashlight in my window before swapping that flashlight for a Breathalyzer, and oh yeah, do you happen to know anything about the guy who was stomped into a vegetable a mile up the road? Witnesses gave a description of said stomper, and it sure as hell resembles you, right down to that little spatter of blood on your shirt.

It was not easy to snuff paranoid prospects like this. They came one after the other like previews before a film. My mind and body hummed with adrenaline. I needed to focus on my breathing if I ever hoped to process this mess.

In for five; hold for five; out for five. And repeat. A few more times. Better now.

What happened to Angela? She was gone when I'd finished with Dickhead, but surely she had to witness *some* of the chaos. Did I scare her? Was she grateful? Chances are she was *initially* grateful, but after witnessing the excessive job I was doing on the guy, she probably freaked and ran off.

I took another deep breath, held it, let it out slow, and began analyzing things as collectively as possible:

I couldn't care less about stomping Dickhead. No regrets there.

I felt justified to step in and protect Angela as she clearly hinted at wanting help with Dickhead. All good there.

So that leaves only one possible explanation: Angela's disappearance was due to my excessive use of force on Dickhead after he was incapacitated. That had to be it.

Shit.

* * *

Two hours had passed, maybe three, who knows. What I do know is that I'd fallen asleep. Shortly after I'd tried to clear my head it began to rain, and the hypnotic sound of rain pelting the roof of my car coupled with the combination of alcohol and spent adrenaline was like a handful of Ambien.

So there I was, passed out in the driver's seat, when those hypnotic drops of rain started to grow louder. The change in noise and tempo sunk in, but sleep still had a good hold of me and wasn't about to let me slip away just yet.

When the rain grew louder still, so loud I can remember a dream where kids were throwing rocks at my car for some reason, I jerked awake to find the imaginary rocks a very real set of knuckles, rapping on my car window.

My whereabouts were a mystery for a brief, frightening moment, and then I saw Angela peering into my car, one hand over her eyes like a visor. I instantly rolled down my window.

"What are you doing?" I said, immediately regretting how curt and accusatory it came out.

I was unsure as to how long she'd been standing there trying to wake me, or how she had even managed to *find* me, but there she stood—hair wet, clothes soaked.

"Are you okay?" she asked with what seemed like sincerity.

I paused for a second, her concern for my well-being making me re-evaluate preconceived notions. I also realized she was still standing in the rain.

"I'm fine. Here—get in." I leaned to my right and opened the passenger door for her.

She obliged my gesture and was soon sitting next to me. The rain had amplified the scents of her hair—some kind of herbal and fruit shampoo I guessed. Whatever it was, it smelled amazing, and made me want to lick every drop of rain off her body.

"I'm really sorry about what happened earlier," I began, deciding to get my bit in first. "I guess I kinda lost it when I saw that guy bothering you like that."

She didn't respond right away. In fact, it didn't even look as though she'd heard me; she seemed transfixed by the endless patterns of rain on the windshield. I questioned whether or not I should repeat myself, and I was just about to when she leaned over and simultaneously kissed me while grabbing my cock.

What should have been a wet dream was handled like a nightmare; her behavior knocked me completely off-guard and caused me to regretfully jump. I didn't need to speak; my befuddled look said it all.

Undeterred, she leaned in again. "That was *so* fucking hot the way you handled that guy. You almost killed him."

I was beyond dumbfounded. " *Hot* ? That whole debacle turned you on?"

"Oh *God*, yes."

"Well, where did you go then? I looked around and you were gone."

"I went for my car. I was planning on coming back for you, but saw you had an admirer."

It took me a second to get the joke. "You mean that girl who was screaming bloody murder?"

"Yeah. She kind of ruined everything."

"She did?"

"Uh-huh." She buried her mouth into my neck. "If she wasn't there, I'd have fucked you right then. In the car. Next to what you'd done."

"Are you serious?"

"*Oh yeah…*"

I had absolutely no clue how to respond to this. *I* was the one who was used to being in control when it came to sexual situations. It was usually *me* that proposed off-the-wall scenarios that were met with looks of uncertainty.

"Does that bother you?" she said, glancing up at me, eyes playing innocent, their true intentions bad, the good kind.

"No," I said softly. And here's the thing: I don't think it *did* bother me. It intrigued me, perhaps for the same reasons my true self had intrigued her. It was the kind of thing I was referring to earlier. What lay behind the beauty? Sex was sex to me, bodies interchangeable. I had no desire to fuck this woman with just my cock; I wanted to fuck her with something as yet untapped; her to fuck me with what seemed like a keen capability to excavate that unexploited relic and make it all virginal, *my first time being fucked* . How the *hell* could this not qualify as therapy?

"Good," she said, lips still to my ear. "Would you like to follow me back to my place?"

"Yes I would."

She pulled away and smirked, confidence everywhere. "I'm going to show you things you won't believe."

THE BAR

The bartender holds up a hand. "Wait—wait, wait, wait. You're not gonna tell me she's a vampire are you?"

Genuinely confused, I say, "What?"

"Getting aroused by violence? Her lips on your neck? *I'm gonna show you things you won't believe'* ?"

I frown. "No, she's not a vampire. Why the hell would I tell you a story about a vampire?"

He shrugs. "Sounded like that's where this was going. My daughter reads all those vampire books. Has the DVDs of the movies playing non-stop."

I sip my Beam. "My condolences."

He grunts in agreement and finishes his second Beam with ice.

I pour him another and he doesn't refuse. I smile.

"Okay," he says, "you're following Angela back to her place…"

PART TWO

THE FREAK

5

I don't remember driving to her house. And I could not, for the life of me, give you even the most rudimentary directions on how to get there; with the potential of what lay ahead, such details had been demoted from steak to vegetables.

In a matter of moments we were on her porch, and, I shit you not, she *kicked* open the front door. Her hand gripping mine, she pulled me up a flight of stairs and led me to a bedroom.

I had not managed, nor had the time or opportunity (or a fucking care) to get a look at the rest of the interior of the house, but the room the two of us now occupied was huge. It's red and black décor suggested eroticism with a devilish taste of the unknown, a kind of danger that entices our better judgment, woos with control and power and all kinds of good wrong.

I barely had a chance to take everything in before Angela was guiding me towards the foot of an enormous bed. She kissed me, sucked on my lower lip as she withdrew, and then shoved me backwards onto the bed where I happily flopped.

She wasted no time in joining me, straddling my waist, undressing the both of us, pausing every now and again to fondle, tantalize, and tease, securing my state of arousal (as if it was going anywhere).

This was brutal anticipation at its best. My entire body throbbed.

We were nearly naked—me in boxers; she in a pair of bra and panties I wanted to eat.

We locked eyes, and then with a flick of her chin she gestured above my head. I followed her gaze, turned and glanced up. A pair of leather wrist wraps dangled across from one another along the headboard. Handcuffs that didn't look like handcuffs. I hadn't noticed them when first flopping on the bed; they too had been demoted to vegetables.

I turned back to Angela, and in a failed effort to control my eagerness, attempted to cut short her performance by reaching up and pulling her to me. My grip was instantly met by hers. She released hold on one of my wrists and wagged a playful finger in my face.

Bad boy, Mr. Court , that waving finger said.

I smiled and let my arms go limp. She began fastening my wrists to the leather cuffs overhead. Finished, she slid off my body (tongue tracing my torso as she did, God bless her) and stood before me at the foot of the bed. She was still wearing her bra and panties, and I took in every inch of her.

I guessed her height at about five-seven, her weight I didn't care to guess; my eyes gifted me with far more than a scale ever could. Full and curved in all the right spots, taught and firm…in all the right spots.

Her hair was shoulder-length and dark, almost black, the color accentuating her blue eyes; lips full and red, her blue eyes accentuating *them*.

Assuming I wasn't still asleep in my car, this was real. I was about to have Angela.

"All good?" she asked, gesturing towards the cuffs that held my wrists overhead.

I could only nod my confirmation—words had no place here. She smiled her approval, and turned her back to me. Slowly, she bent and removed her panties, revealing an ass you wanted to bite, and kiss, and slap, and bite…

An uncontrollable spasm of anticipation hit me and I inadvertently tugged on the cuffs overhead—and my right wrist nearly popped free. Turns out the cuff was loose and not properly fastened.

Her back still to me, Angela had not noticed my incident with the loose cuff, and I sure as *hell* wasn't about to let her notice lest she stop her performance to re-fasten the stupid thing. So I simply held my hand in a fixed position as though the cuff on my right was as tight as the one on my left. As long as I didn't do anything stupid like that again, I figured I'd be okay.

Once her panties had been removed, Angela went to work on her bra, glancing over her shoulder at me as she did so. The look she cast me was something no surgeon could ever provide, a confidence I'd never seen in any woman, like she damn well knew she could make you come with just her eyes. The next time someone tells you it's big tits or a tight ass, scoff; nothing is sexier than the elusive trait of true confidence.

The bra was off. She turned slowly and faced me, her arms across her chest, a hand covering each breast. It seemed illogical that she would cover her breasts while everything else was exposed (and looking fucking amazing FYI), but logic had no place in Angela's world. And while men usually accommodated the breasts in order to get further below, I found myself wanting nothing more than to just *see* her breasts, even if it meant I might never get to touch, taste, or enter her where I'd always presumed it counted.

The power. The *power* this woman had. She was turning out to be everything I'd been pining for.

My state of arousal was now higher than it had ever been. I wanted her on the bed with me. Nothing else mattered. Nothing else existed. This strange room was my whole world and Angela and I were the only two people alive.

Or so I thought.

Something caught my attention to the right of me. About fifteen feet from the bed, a pair of long, red drapes hung and cloaked what I assumed was some kind of panoramic window. What made these drapes catch my attention at a time when very little else *could* catch my attention, was that I was sure I saw something move behind them.

Angela, reading my face, turned and joined me in staring at the drapes, hands still covering her breasts.

"Now," she said.

I looked at her, and then immediately back at the drapes as a man stepped out from behind them. At least I think it was a man. Hell, it had to be; he was huge. The rest of his appearance was far too bizarre to initially comprehend. He donned a full-body get-up; tight to the skin and all black, like something a villain in a comic book might wear. His face was covered by a mask that looked to be fashioned out of the same tight-fitting black material as his body suit. There were holes for the eyes, nose, and mouth, but they were covered in circles of black mesh—nothing identifiable to the onlooker; vision, air, and a voice for the one wearing the mask.

I found myself almost laughing at the flagrant absurdity of it all. I wanted Angela to take me to places as yet untapped, but this...

Chuckling I said, "What the f—?" but stopped when I saw this freak pull an aluminum bat out from behind his leg. Hardly chuckling now: "What the *fuck* ?"

As if my words were a starting pistol, the freak let out a deafening battle cry and rocketed towards the bed, bat cocked and ready. I quickly rolled to the left, my right wrist that hadn't been properly fastened to the cuff breaking free, allowing me out of harm's way.

Thank *God* I never mentioned the fucking thing.

The bat clanged off the headboard a mere two inches from my head. I rolled off the bed completely and began frantically working on the remaining cuff that held my left wrist. The cuff was held on by the same mechanism you might attach a leather belt, and the pulling I'd just done caused a good deal of tension to accumulate, tightening the bond. I needed to loosen the slack.

To my right, the freak was regrouping, cautiously circling the bed, securing his grip on the bat. I could hear him breathing, excited. I backed up further against the wall and felt my right hand graze something. I glanced down at a sizeable porcelain lamp on a nightstand.

He finished circling the bed. We now faced each other, maybe eight feet apart, the bat swaying over his shoulder as though waiting for a pitch.

Another battle cry and another charge. He vaulted forward, bat cocked. I spun, snatched the lamp by its neck, spun back and whipped it into his oncoming face. It shattered on impact, knocking him backwards, out cold.

Ignoring all of my mother's childhood advice, I decided to use my teeth as a tool, spinning back towards the bed and chomping down onto the leather strap that held my wrist captive, hoping to loosen the slack. It worked, and I now had my left hand back.

Good thing too. The freak was awake and on his feet.

He'd dropped the bat after I cracked him with the lamp, and for some reason did not attempt to grab it again. There was a good chance he was still on queer street from the lamp and wasn't thinking properly, and to be honest, I didn't give a shit; the fact that he was no longer wielding the thing gave me hope.

The freak dove at my waist, shooting both of us backwards, crashing against the wall. Although the impact momentarily took my breath, I was happy the wall was there; it kept me upright and prevented me from landing on my back with his big ass on top.

With his shoulder driving into my stomach, I felt him reach down to grab the back of my legs so that he could scoop me up and slam me. Fuck that. I immediately took both hands and pushed down onto the back of his head until it was at my knees, preventing him from getting any leverage. I then snaked one of my legs free, and began hammering the bottom of my fist onto the back of his head like a jackhammer. After about five or six of those, he gave up trying to slam me and covered up.

I snaked my other leg free, clamped both hands around his neck, and drove my knee up into his face with everything I had. It sounded like a football being punted. He dropped instantly.

I slumped back against the wall. My lungs burned. My body shook. I was certain I was going to puke. And then I felt a frantic pull on one of my ankles.

I looked down and actually gasped: "*Are you fucking kidding me?*"

The tough fucker was now clamped onto my shin. His fingers groped and clawed my flesh as he tried to climb to his feet.

I spotted the discarded bat. Picked it up and raised it overhead.

Although he never looked up, I now suspect the freak realized what was about to happen; he stopped his futile struggle at my legs and seemed to brace himself for the inevitable.

I could have stopped after the first blow (he went limp immediately), but I didn't. In retrospect, I can think of many reasons—some reasonable, if not damn well justifiable—as to why I didn't, but who cares, right?

I didn't.

Over and over again I brought the bat down onto the freak's masked skull, deforming it with each sickening wallop.

It was my breath—or lack thereof—that finally stopped me. Realization as to what I'd done soon began filtering into my pool of rage and I instantly flung the bat into the corner where it landed with a definitive clang.

I looked down at the now lifeless mass at my feet. His body was still moving, but it was involuntary, just a convulsive twitch or two until he was officially a corpse.

A corpse.

He was dead. The guy was fucking *dead* . And I'd killed him. I had *killed* somebody. This wasn't just pummeling someone in a street fight. This was murder. Yes, I'd acted in self-defense, but I was excessive and I knew it and the result was still the same. Death—by me.

What to do? I had to get away. Leave.

Wait a minute.

Angela. Where the hell was Angela? My head whipped all over the room. I saw nothing.

She must still be in the house though, right? After all, this *was* her house, wasn't it? She wouldn't be stupid enough to leave me alone here would she?

Maybe you're not alone, I thought. *Maybe there are more people in the house. More people like the freak.*

This terrifying prospect stopped me from calling her name and made an immediate exit priority one.

I quickly gathered my stuff and darted from the room. Gripping the railing, I took the stairs two at a time until I was at the front door, still ajar from when Angela had kicked it open and for a split-second I marveled at how relative time could be. Mere minutes ago I nearly came in my pants when she kicked that door open. Now I feared I might shit them.

For the second time this evening, I was in my car and speeding away from a barbaric scene I'd committed.

THE BAR

"So you're saying you killed the guy?" the bartender asks.

I take a healthy pull on my whiskey and nod as I swallow.

The bartender waves a hand in front of my mangled face. "But he didn't do all that to you…"

"No."

"So who did?"

I drain my Beam and pour myself another. The trodden boards of *Fuck It* are now getting soaked. I smile at the bartender, my buzz teetering over the line of drunk, and hold up a finger. "Patience, my friend," I say.

I'm happy to see a subtle roll of his eyes. As I'd predicted, he has already started labeling me as a drunken bull-shitter, my injuries the probable result of an excessive beating at the hands of a few douche bags at some other watering hole the night before. And like I said; that's just fine by me—it's better if he doesn't believe. Because everything I just told him was a fucking cake-walk compared to what was in store for me.

6

I drove aimlessly until I had a general idea of where I was. Before long, I was on a recognizable route home.

The severities of the previous hour's events played on a continuous loop inside my head. I had romanticized committing murder during dark times before, usually drunk, but always within the guarded perimeter of my delusional mind. Whether I knew deep down that I was full of shit, I don't know; it was irrelevant now, wasn't it? Tonight, the guarded perimeter had been breached—my delusional mind had had its bluff called in a big fucking way, and now it was on the run, desperate to find somewhere to hole up so it could plan its next move.

The police? No way. I'd had a few run-ins with the police in my day, mostly stupid shit—bar fights, the majority—that concluded with a slap on the wrist or a night in a cell until I sobered up, yet I now looked at the police as an absolute last resort. I had a horrifying fear of prison, permanently warped from the abundance of cable documentaries I'd seen about prison life. I may be able to handle myself in a scrap or two, but I had no delusions of what would happen to a suburban white boy like me if I went to Graterford prison.

What I needed to do was find Angela. She was the only one who had witnessed the event, and she was the only one who could answer the multitude of questions I had. After all, this whole debacle could have very well been her doing. One minute she's about to screw me (or so I thought), and the next she's saying "Now" to some freak in black leather jammies so he could start a swingin' with a fucking baseball bat.

Yeah—she definitely had some explaining to do, the crazy bitch. Her desire for sex next to the guy I'd stomped outside the bar should have been one hell of a red flag, but my insistence on a stupid expedition for that virginal relic had made me all but color-blind.

It was now perfectly clear that finding Angela was the most logical first course of action. Problem was, the clock on my dashboard read five-thirty a.m., and my body was pushed to the limits of exhaustion. Although the suggestion seemed absurd considering recent events, I needed to sleep, if only for a few hours so that I could recharge and regroup. I decided to head home.

7

As I put my key into my apartment door, I knew I would be greeted by a pissed-off cat. I had missed his dinner time by almost twelve hours. Inexcusable. Anyone who has ever owned a cat will tell you they like routine. Break that routine, and you can get anything from a 3 a.m. siren in your ear, to a stink-wrapped gift waiting for you on your rug. Fortunately, I did not receive the latter, but I did receive a siren job as I entered my apartment.

Pele, named after mixed martial arts legend Jose "Pele" Landi-Jons, is all black with yellow eyes. He's an awesome cat that I'm convinced was a badass panther in a past life.

I was too tired, dazed, scared, paranoid, (hell, all-of-the-fucking-above) to bend and scoop him up for a cuddle like I normally did when I got home. Good thing too—as late as I was with his dinner, he might have swiped me a good one if I tried.

Instead I just lumbered into the kitchen with Pele hot on my heels. He immediately leapt onto the kitchen counter and began circling the electric can opener with all the patience of a junkie needing a fix.

I opened a can of cat food, the whir of the machine a duet with his anxious meows, then plopped the contents into a bowl and lowered it to the floor. In a second, half of his head was in the bowl, devouring with that little growl he sometimes made when he meant business. Ordinarily, this made me smile. Not today.

I began undressing on the way to my bedroom, clothes tossed and landing where they landed. I needed to sleep; my body begged for it. I would have to begin my search for Angela tomorrow, or should I say, later today. *Then* I would get some answers. Nothing I could do about it now. What's done is done.

(*Yeah, you keep telling yourself that, killer.*)

8

Somehow, I managed to find some sleep. When I woke, there was a heavy weight on my chest that I initially expected to be my old friend anxiety, but turned out to be Pele. He had obviously forgiven me for missing dinner, and was now curled up and sawing wood on my sternum. I hated to wake him, but one more minute and I would have asphyxiated, so I kept nudging him until he reluctantly opened his eyes and nipped at my hand.

"Come on—off," I said.

One more nudge and he took the hint, but not without casting me his best *when you least expect it...* glare before hopping off the bed.

My clock read one thirty p.m. I got up and began trudging around my apartment, picking clothes off the floor or out of my hamper that could be worn a second day. I certainly wasn't going to wear what I had on last night. No blood had sprayed or stained anything (I recommend killing all people in your underwear—very economical), but putting them back on was out of the question. I needed no reminders for what I'd done, thank you.

I happened upon a T-shirt with no stains that smelled decent, and an old pair of jeans that could go through a shit storm and still pass for acceptable. Dressed, I then entered my den and stood.

What now? My stomach burbled. It was anxiety, but I did need food. I had all day and night to find Angela as I was not due into work until the next day, so maybe I could figure shit out over lunch. Hunker down somewhere, get my thoughts together, chase my lunch with a pitcher of whiskey and fifty Xanax.

No. Forget food; I needed to deal with this shit now. I wouldn't have been able to get anything down my throat anyway. Anything that wasn't at least 80-proof, that is.

I went back into my bedroom, scooped up my car keys, wallet, my Yankees hat (not a Yankees fan, or even a baseball fan, but my buddy Paul gave it to me), and then hurried out my apartment.

As I walked through the outdoor lot of my building, I noticed something resting on the windshield of my car, about thirty yards ahead. I squinted on approach. It looked like someone's purse. As I got closer, I noted that it was not a purse, but a random piece of black clothing. I picked the material up, fanned it out, and found myself staring at the same mask the freak had been wearing last night.

"Boo!"

I spun and nearly lost my balance. Angela stood before me, giggling. She reached out and began petting my cheek as she spoke.

"Aww... poor baby. Did I scare you?"

I stared at her blankly while my mind worked for a response. She continued.

"No early bird special for you, sleepy-head. It's almost two."

Still no capable response on my part. She was acting as if last night's events were a simple date between the two of us.

"Calvin? You okay?"

All I could do was thrust the mask into her chest. She took it and gave the thing a glance of mild interest.

"You're lucky I cleaned it before giving it to you," she said. "It was pretty gross when I took it off."

" *Giving it to me?* " I said. "Why the hell would you give this to me?"

"Well, seeing as I've got an immediate opening, I figured you'd be the perfect candidate," she said, her tone still pleasant and unassuming, like we were discussing where to go for lunch.

My head spun. Her words were clear and concise, but I may as well have been deaf for all the sense they were making. She placed the mask back into my hands and, by reflex, I accepted her offering before dropping it a split-second later. Her head dropped with the mask and she eyed it for a moment.

"I don't blame you," she said. "I wouldn't want to wear a used one either. We'll get you fitted for a new one."

"Angela," I began, finally gathering up a fraction of my wits, "I'm pretty sure I killed that guy."

"Yes, Calvin, I know," she said, sarcasm light but there.

"Did you do it?" I asked.

"No—you did it."

"No, I mean did you *do it* ? Did you set it up? Did you *plan* it?"

She gave a sly raise of her eyebrow. "How do you feel?"

"What?"

"How do you *feel* ?"

"How the fuck do you think I feel?"

She smiled. "You *are* feeling something though, right?"

I knew what she was getting at.

"Yes I am" —my turn with the sarcasm— "however, your method of hands-on therapy seems a bit fucking radical, wouldn't you say?"

"I wouldn't say," she replied. "Who am I to say what's right and wrong? You acted with the most primitive of instincts and temporarily discarded that labyrinth you call a mind."

I didn't respond, but she continued like a professor lecturing a class.

"We're animals, Calvin, all of us. What are the drives that shape an animal's life?"

I frowned, confused. "Huh?"

"Eating, sleeping, fucking, and killing. They don't ask permission; they just do. Do we chastise their behavior?"

"You can't be serious. They're *animals* . They don't have morals or the ability to rationalize the way we do."

"And where do morals come from? Are you so naïve as to think they are inherent? Hard-wired to us in the womb?"

"No, but I'm not about to try and teach a fucking lion the pitfalls of killing with impunity."

She chuckled at my remark and said: "And yet we share their impulses. Shame."

I shook my head. "Bullshit. I'll give you eating and sleeping and sex, but killing? That's not a drive. That's not an impulse. At least not for normal people."

"Isn't it? Or has society buried that impulse so deep throughout the centuries that no amount of conscious digging can unearth it?"

I shrugged. "Whatever, professor. I just know it's not an impulse for me."

She smirked with a creepy confidence. "Ooooh…liar, liar."

I just stared at her. She stared back with her confident smirk. I'm ashamed to admit it, but for a brief moment I began researching her previous inquiry: *Was* I feeling? Yes, but what exactly was it? Panic? Check. Anxiety? Check. Paranoia? Check. But who governed these feelings? Was the ruler someone who ticked those boxes because he took another man's life, or were those boxes ticked by a governor bred with a fear of getting caught? A fear of prison? It was disturbing that the answer—at least the one I hoped for; the one about taking a man's life—did not come so readily. But, Jesus, my actions weren't born through drive or impulse. They weren't.

(*Did a number on him though, didn't ya? Maybe if you'd stopped after the first hit, he wouldn't have died.*)

"I don't know what you want me to say," I said, shaking away that last thought that came at me like a bullet.

"I can help you, Calvin."

"With what?"

"Alex was talking too much. What we do requires exceptional discretion. You handled the problem with Alex brilliantly. You also proved that you were more than qualified to fill his shoes."

So many questions.

I started with: "Who the hell is Alex?"

The smirk again. "The guy you played baseball with last night."

So now the freak had a name. I liked it better when he was just a freak.

"'Qualified to fill his shoes'? 'Exceptional discretion'? You can 'help me'? I'm not following any of this—at all."

"I think it would be best if I showed you."

"The last time you said you were going to show me something I ended up bashing a guy's head in with a baseball bat."

She inched close. Got on her toes and tried to kiss me. I grabbed her shoulders and pulled away.

"What the hell is wrong with you?" I said.

She shrugged, her face now indifferent. "Suit yourself. I was just offering a signing bonus. Didn't think you'd waive it." She turned and started walking away. "Someone will be in touch."

I glanced down at the discarded mask. I glanced back up at Angela, strolling towards a black Mercedes with tinted windows.

"Wait!" I called. I hadn't planned it; the word seemed to leap out on its own. I was just so ridiculously confused. And her parting words: *Someone will be in touch* . Someone like who? Another freak maybe? And in touch for what?

Angela stopped at her driver door, turned and faced me. She was maybe ten yards away, close enough to read that indifferent face of hers. Close enough to read that indifferent face shifting ever so slightly into one waiting for more from me, perhaps a tad impatient now because I'd rebuffed her advances.

I wanted to hear whatever there was to hear from *her* ; not wait in my apartment until someone else came knocking.

"Wait," I said again. "I'm coming."

She nodded, even-faced, and motioned to the passenger side of the Mercedes. "Hop in."

PART THREE

FOR YOUR VIEWING PLEASURE

9

The drive to wherever we were going was curiously quiet. Angela didn't offer much in the way of conversation, and my mind was going in all directions, trying to predict what lay in store for me. One of those predictions was soon answered as the route towards our destination began to look familiar. We were heading back to the house where I'd killed the freak.

A shot of adrenaline swirled in my belly as we ultimately pulled into the long driveway. I wondered if the freak—what did she say his name was? Alex?—would be where I left him. Angela had removed his mask, but had she moved his body? He was a big guy. Did she have help? I remembered bolting from the house after killing the freak at the thought of *more* freaks lurking in the house. Was my intuition justified? *Were* there more inside—waiting? I didn't care how badly I wanted answers; I had no desire to fight for my life on a regular basis to accommodate this woman. I told her so.

"Angela, wait."

She was already making her way towards the front door; I was still by the car. She stopped and turned. My mouth opened, but I didn't have the words. Fortunately, I didn't need them; my face seemed to say it all.

She smiled. "Relax, sexy. Last time was just a test." She then winked and added: "I left that cuff loose on purpose ya know."

* * *

Inside, Angela led me towards an extravagant living room, something you'd see in a magazine for the uber-rich. Even my ignorance wagered I could snag any of the dozens of antiques throughout, make a run for it, and be set for life after I hawked the thing.

Angela took my hand and guided me towards one of those cozy plush chairs that look like a giant marshmallow waiting to swallow you. I happily obliged its appetite and sank into the cushy material, helpless to the sigh that followed. Nervous or not, the thing was damn comfy. Angela then heightened my comfort by placing a drink in my hand immediately after, as if it'd already been poured and ready before our arrival.

Others in the house?

I studied the drink's color in the short crystal glass. Smelled it. Felt my tongue and throat beckon for confirmation. And then took a sip and confirmed all hope—single malt scotch as smooth and as tasty as I imagined Angela herself.

This was not the type of drink you were in a hurry to finish, but like the cartoon owl in that old Tootsie Pop commercial, my palate had no patience in discovering how many licks it took to get to the center. Three quick swallows and it was gone.

"Good?" Angela asked.

"Very," I said.

"Want another?"

I did. I really, really did. Except something deep inside—despite all protests from the pleasure center—told me not to. After last night's events, I had a keen sense I would need my wits about me, not have them dulled by alcohol. I didn't care about any of her assurances that all was well and that last night was just a test, whatever the hell that meant. I wanted to be sober and alert.

"Yes…" I said. "But no."

"No? It's one of the finest single malts in the entire—"

"I know it's good," I said. "No thank you."

She shrugged, said, "Suit yourself," and then headed towards a cabinet the size of a garage door at the far-end of the living room.

A few clicks and turns of the locks on those big cabinet doors and she soon swung them open. Inside the cabinet was a screen more apt for a movie theater than a living room. The base of the screen sported an array of technology that, again, seemed more apt for a movie theater than a home. The only things I recognized were multiple DVD players and speakers, each of them capable of ruining your credit rating with a mere glance.

Angela took a remote from the base of the set, backed away a few feet, pointed and clicked some buttons. A giant blue screen awaiting instruction waited.

"You ready?" she asked, smiling eagerly.

"Sure," I said with a sudden indifference that was actually genuine. At this rate, I didn't think anything was capable of shocking me.

Angela pushed play. What I saw shocked the living hell out of me.

THE BAR

"So what was on the TV?" the bartender asks.

"You're one of those guys who skips to the last page of a book, aren't you?" I say, my words beginning to slur.

He doesn't say anything, just fills my glass with more Beam: more story.

"That single malt of hers was fucking amazing," I say. "You got anything like that here?"

The bartender snorts and waves an arm over the place. "What do *you* think?"

Yeah—dumb question. Still: "Well what's the closest you got?"

He pushes off the edge of the bar, casts me a tired look, then turns and begins clanking bottles around as he searches one of the top shelves.

"Holy shit," he says, back still to me.

"What?"

He turns back, holding a bottle like it's a baby. "Macallan 18 Year. How the hell did this get here?"

It's no nectar of the gods, but it's a damn fine scotch. "Fuck yeah— crack it open, man."

He cradles his baby, shielding it from me. "You nuts? This has gotta be a mistake. Joe wouldn't have stocked this."

"It's on the shelf," I say. "Fair game, yeah?"

"This stuff goes for almost two hundred a bottle."

I groan with all the subtlety of a teenager's fart, dig into my pocket, and slap four hundred on the bar. "You can replace the bottle, and then buy your *own*. Plus, I'll let you drink this one with me."

He looks at the money, the bottle, me. The money, the bottle, me. The money, the bottle—

"What's to figure out?" I say. "It's a fucking no-brainer."

"Fuck it," he says, cracking the bottle, grabbing two new glasses, and of course, taking my money.

"Atta boy," I say.

He pours—two modest neats. We raise our glasses to our noses, close our eyes, and breathe in. We sip, exhale, smile.

"Might not be as good as Angela's," I say, "but that's a damn fine scotch."

He only nods, taking another sniff, but not sipping.

I look at the half-empty bottle of Beam, pick it up and toss it over my shoulder. It shatters and the bartender is jerked from his bouquet.

"Hey!" he says.

"It was upsetting the Macallan."

"Yeah, well, I'm the one who's gonna have to clean that up."

I wave a hand in front of him as though the idea of thinking that far ahead is ludicrous.

"Live for the moment, man," I say. "I didn't think I ever could, but…"

I trail off, my mind replaying the recent events of my life like someone randomly skipping chapters on a DVD.

The bartender asks: "You alright?"

I snap from my daze, nod, give the gruesome smile, drain my scotch and say, "Encore."

He fills my glass. "Please don't break anything else."

I laugh. "Promise." I sip, savor, swallow, and say: "Wanna know what she showed me?"

10

I watched in disbelief. What I saw couldn't have been real. I didn't look away until the end, yet my memory of it all remains fragmented. An unconscious defense mechanism for the mind to prevent insanity overload maybe.

Fragment number one:

A bird's-eye view of a guy strapped to an operating table. A beast of a man, not unlike the freak (outfit and all), cutting into the abdomen of the guy on the table. The cuts were not crude; they were meticulous, purposeful. The man on the table was being dissected, each item removed and placed carefully in a metal tray next to him at eye-level…so he could watch. No anesthesia for this guy. Gagged, moaning, crying, he was bearing witness to his literal unravelling.

Fragment number two:

A man shackled to a wall. Gagged and nude. Another beast of a man was at the helm, although his outfit was different. No full-body black suit and mask. He wore tattered jeans, no shirt, and what looked like an executioner's hood. Unlike fragment one, this beast was destroying his man from the outside in.

He started with the fingers. One by one with his bare hands. Snap, snap, snap, and so on. I looked at the floor when he did the man's knees. A sledgehammer to both. When I looked up, the shackled man was unconscious, the pain likely too much, causing a shutdown. The executioner took this as his cue to call it a wrap, to use the sledge on the man's head. It took only one swing. What remained of the man's head was unrecognizable.

Fragment number three:

An iron maiden. One of those medieval torture devices that look like a coffin stood upright. Except instead of a cushy lining for an interior, there's an array of thick spikes from top to bottom looking to poke some serious holes in any unfortunate who was forced inside. And there was an unfortunate, of course.

I watched this unfortunate, bound appropriately to make it work (getting an unbound man inside an iron maiden was, I imagined, like getting Pele into his pet carrier for the vet), shoved inside, and kept watching as they slammed the spiked door shut. But when they slowly opened it? Revealing the aftermath of the unfortunate therein? That was when I finally looked away for good.

I felt Angela's stare on me throughout it all. She seemed to be watching my reaction more than the TV. When I finally turned my head from the screen, she spared me and switched it off.

"What are you thinking?" she asked.

I stared at her. In the last few hours, and especially in the last few minutes, I doubted my own existence. I believed that what I was feeling was too surreal for what goes on in real life. Angela was right: I *was* feeling, but I had not planned on feeling with no warning. I pictured it a slow, grueling process that would one day present itself with all of the immediateness of gray hair. This was thrust onto me with the suddenness of a hiccup.

"Well?" she persisted.

"Was that real?" seemed like the thing to say.

"It's real."

"Why did you show me these?"

"Why do you think?"

"I'm afraid to tell you what I think."

"Well then maybe you've figured it out."

"You said you had an immediate opening. Last night was a test. I was a perfect candidate."

"Wait for it…"

"You want me to be one of the freaks in your videos. One of the guys in the mask."

"Give the man a cigar."

"You want me to torture people for your enjoyment."

She put a hand on her chest. " *My* enjoyment?" Her hand left her chest as she splayed both. " *Everyone's* enjoyment."

"What?"

"Come on, Calvin. I'll admit I've got a fetish or two, but I'm not stupid enough to take a risk like this if I didn't have the promise of security and financial gain."

"Financial gain? Are you telling me you *sell* these videos? There's a market for shit like this?"

"Oh God yeah. You'd be shocked at some of the clientele I have. Celebrities, politicians…. That's why discretion is so important."

"This…this is very fucked up."

"Oh, come on, Calvin. What happened to that dark side of yours?" I didn't respond.

"Do you think what's happened here is by accident? It's my *job* to find people like you. To find people who are lost and have no direction and who have a genuine distaste for the very world that houses them. Do you think I just wandered into your spa for a massage one day by chance?"

I stared at her like a kid slapped.

"Every day on your lunch break you go to the food court at the mall. And every day you order your food and sit as far away from people as you can. *Everybody* people watches, Calvin—but not you. No, you keep your head down and pressed into a magazine or a book or even the surface of the table—God forbid you should make eye contact with someone.

"When you're done eating, you head to the DVD store and make a beeline towards the horror movies. You thumb through them, consider a few, but usually never buy; you just like to look. I always saw this pacifying look of contentment when you thumbed through those movies..."

"Lots of horror fans out there. Doesn't make me Ted Bundy."

She smiled. "That's true. What sold me on you was the kid."

"The kid?"

"You'd just finished your lunch one day. You were reading something—a horror movie magazine I believe?" She smirked and I looked away. "Anyway," she said, "you were reading your magazine when a little boy ran by your table and tripped. He skidded on his face and really hurt himself. Everyone in the vicinity gasped in horror and concern. They immediately went to the child's aid. But not you. What did you do, Calvin? Do you remember?"

I felt my chest tighten.

"You laughed didn't you? Well, you *wanted* to laugh. Slapped your hand over your mouth and did your absolute damnedest not to burst out on the spot."

I remembered. I *did* stifle a laugh.

"The boy was really hurt. His face was bloodied. Yet I never saw a look of concern on your face. I saw...what did I see? Was it gratification? Enjoyment maybe?" She paused deliberately, her smirk now painted on. "Do you remember this?"

"I remember."

"Ninety-nine percent of the people who witnessed that child fall were upset and concerned, yet you wanted to laugh. That's why you're here."

My chest continued to shrink. I had always been aware of my shortcomings and issues, but I had no idea that I would end up being the subject of someone's study of which to utilize these undesirables. How the hell could I? I decided to voice some reason.

"Watching a kid trip and fall is one thing. Watching someone being systematically tortured is another. A *big* fucking other."

"Or maybe you were just the only one with the balls to laugh in public."

I shook my head in protest. "I'm not proud of it. I—if the kid was like, *badly* hurt I wouldn't have wanted to laugh."

She ignored me as if I'd said nothing. "Look at television," she began. "It's all *about* violence. The media, TV drama, even comedy. Have you seen those internet shows of people doing stupid shit and getting seriously hurt? The audience roars. We *all* have a morbid fascination with violence. Problem is, society castrates us; instills us with those holier-than-thou morals that repress these needs and wants. It gives but doesn't approve. Can you fathom a bigger hypocrisy?"

"Again, you're comparing a stupid kid falling off his skateboard and squashing his nuts to people being brutally tortured. The first *is* funny; the latter is not. Like I said, if the little boy at the mall had been *badly* hurt, I wouldn't have—"

"He *was* badly hurt."

"You don't know that."

"Neither do you."

Dammit.

"It's nothing new, Calvin. It's not Marilyn Manson or Metallica's fault we're this way. Christ, public executions used to be a social event. Families showed up for them. Kids.

"The problem is that most people aren't willing to embrace these needs and wants. My clientele is. They've not only come to terms with these impulses, but managed to turn them into a shameless fetish that will fulfill every desire that society shuns."

" *Fucking crazy,* " I muttered.

"Why do people slow down when passing a car accident?" she asked.

I made a face. "The police maybe?"

She gave me a look. "Don't insult me."

I knew what she was getting at. Of course people slow for the police, but there's another reason. Damn if I'd give her the satisfaction of voicing it though.

"Everybody wants to look," she said, voicing it for me. "Everybody looks in hopes of getting a glimpse of that mangled body. Later they'll re-tell the event, say how tragic, how horrible, but deep down, that suppressed urge—be it conscious or unconscious—tasted delight in that glimpse."

I still didn't respond. She was making sense and it disturbed me.

"Let me ask you something," she said. "Now that it's done, how do you feel after last night?"

"You already asked me that."

"And I don't recall a definitive answer."

I said nothing.

"Are you really so distraught that you took another man's life?" she said. "Or are you conflicted because you don't feel remorse about what you did? You *think* it should bother you, it's *not* bothering you, and *that's* what's bothering you."

I twitched. "How can you say it's not bothering me? How would you know? How would you know *anything* about me? All you've got to go on is what we've said to each other during half a dozen massage sessions."

"I can certainly judge you from what I've recently seen."

"What I did last night was self-defense."

"A bit excessive wasn't it? What about the poor guy at the bar?"

"I was defending *you* !"

She made the kind of face people make when they see a puppy. "I know. That was so sweet. So predictable."

Predictable?

"Did you have something to do with that too?" I said.

She winked at me. "Your psycho act cost me an additional three grand. I had to visit the guy at the hospital the next day to pay him. We had no idea you were gonna be so rough."

"I don't believe this...you've been playing me like a fucking..." I stopped and dropped my head into my hands. "Those movies...I can't believe you produce and sell shit like that."

"Well, I'm not the only one," she said.

I lifted my head. "What do you mean? You saying you have competitors?"

"Of course I do. I'm the biggest though. Well...second biggest. I *do* think I'm the best. Soon I'll be the best *and* the biggest."

"Who's number one?" I asked.

"Whoa, easy there, sexy; I wouldn't use the term *number one* . They're just *bigger* . They have a larger clientele because they deal in sick shit."

"Dare I ask what you classify as *sick shit* ?"

"Bestiality; couples pissing and shitting on each other; gang rape." She sneered. "Sick."

"Well it's nice to know morality isn't *totally* lost on people of your ilk."

"Funny. So you want the job?"

"Think I'll have to pass," I said.

"It was kind of a rhetorical question."

"How's that?"

"Well you don't have much of a say in the matter do you? It's a bit late to start changing your decision at this stage of the game."

"I never *made* any decision."

"You made your decision when you killed Alex," she said.

"You gotta be kidding me. That guy came at me like a fucking maniac."

"Really?" she said, her face a bad actor's try at quizzical. "I don't remember it that way."

She pushed a few more buttons on the remote. I heard the whir of the

DVD player changing discs. The TV came to life again.

It was me. Killing the freak. The whole thing caught on tape from multiple points of view.

Strike that. It was *not* the whole thing.

It did not show Angela.

It did not show me bound on the bed.

It did not show the freak emerging from behind the curtains with an aluminum bat, charging, wanting to take my head off.

It showed me bludgeoning a man to death.

It showed a close-up of my panting face.

It showed a close-up of the twitching, very dead freak.

Never mind the freak was dressed in a black Spiderman getup. Never mind I was wearing nothing but boxer shorts. The way the film had been edited, we could have been two kinky lovers doing a little role-playing before yours truly took it a bit too far.

Bottom line: the film made me look like a stone-cold killer.

I stared at the black screen for several beats after Angela clicked it off. I could see my reflection in that screen. I looked small, like the once-cozy marshmallow chair *was* swallowing me. I wished it would.

"I assume that was a copy?" I managed to say.

"Yeah. Why, did you want one?"

I glared at her.

"So this is some kind of blackmail," I said.

"Ugly word."

"But apt," I said. "Problem is, if you turn me in, I'll turn you in. I'll tell them everything about you. You might have doctored that footage to make me look guilty, but with the right lawyer…"

"You could do that," she replied. "You'd be taking a pretty big chance though."

"How so?"

"I've been doing this a long time, Calvin. I've got all the necessary wheels greased. Like I said, you'd be absolutely stunned if you knew who some of my clients were."

I could feel my pulse in my head.

She kneeled before me, reached up and stroked my cheek. "Look at that handsome face." She brought her hand down into the chair's plush material and gripped my ass. "Look at that tight little ass. Do you know what would happen to someone like you in prison, Calvin?"

She had hit on one my strongest phobias. My reply was barely above a whisper. "Yes," I mumbled.

"It would be a tragedy to let such a wonderful man go to waste." She unbuttoned my pants, pulled them to my ankles.

My dick in her hand, mouth closing in, she glanced up at me with predatory eyes. "Don't worry, baby…it's going to be a fun ride."

11

The next two hours were spent in bed. I'd never had a woman fuck me like that before. Never. It wasn't so much the physical stuff she did—though it was all there, and top-shelf indeed—but the *way* she did it. I said it earlier and I'll say it again, the one thing I'll never understand about women is all the time and money spent on improving the shell, when in reality the hottest thing about a woman is confidence. Sure, the shell matters—no "beauty is only skin deep" preaching here—but the shell can crack. Nothing will ever crack true confidence, often imitated by the arrogant, often plagiarized by the insecure. True confidence is a wonderful trip indeed, and Angela gave me the grand tour she did she did.

She also had the decency to bring me to a different room than the one I had "played baseball" in, to which I was very grateful. I never did remember to ask her if the freak's body was still in the house somewhere. Part of me didn't want to. Because if it was gone, disposed of, then that heightened my anxiety of help being close by. That freak was a big, tough fucker—which likely meant there were more big, tough fuckers floating around. Maybe the first test was over, but maybe I had eight more innings ahead of me. Who the hell knew? The only thing I did know was that the woman was human Xanax; those worries receded the entire time we were together. Murder? Blackmail? Future employee of Dahmer's Wet Dreams, Inc.? Petty stuff when Angela's having her way with you.

Except we were done now, my body drained of fluid, but plentiful again with fear and apprehension. I was also drained of food. I hadn't eaten yet today, and my stomach was talking. Angela, who had been dozing on my belly, lifted her head, yawned and said, "Are you hungry?"

"Yeah," I said. "I haven't eaten yet today."

I expected her to offer me something, or perhaps suggest we go out together for a bite. But all she did was roll off the bed and head for the bathroom. I figured she wanted to use the toilet. Be back in a minute after a quick pee with a proposal for food. Instead I heard the shower.

Okay, I thought. *A quick pee and a shower. That's cool—I can wait.*

Nope.

Angela opened the bathroom door a crack, her disembodied voice loud over the running water.

"You can go, Calvin," she said. "I'll call you when I need you."

She closed the door and I soon heard the rhythm of the shower change as her body hit the water. I remained on the bed, naked and confused. Her indifference to our recent passion was both curious and humbling. I sat up and swung my legs over the side of the bed, trying to work it out. Was it all just business? My ego wanted to believe that at least some of her intensity was genuine, but for all I knew, this was part of her *job* , and I was simply another freak's cock that needed milking.

Still, my ego insisted there was something else there. Not much, but something. Maybe. Something?

(*No. Now can we go eat?*)

I sighed and got dressed. I patted my pants' pockets for my keys, then checked the two nightstands. I was about to drop to my hands and knees and start searching the floor when I remembered Angela had driven me here. My car was back at my apartment.

I felt nervous knocking on the bathroom door. I had just spent the last two hours screwing this woman all over the freaking bedroom, and now I was worried about bothering her in the shower? Again, the power this woman possessed...

I rapped lightly on the door. She didn't answer. I rapped louder. Her response was firm.

"What?"

I stuttered before I spoke, embarrassed and cursing myself for it. "I have no car," I said.

"What?"

I opened the door a crack. Steam hit me and I could just make out her nude silhouette behind the fogged glass walls of her shower. Although I was reasonably certain that I had no semen left in my body, I wanted nothing more than to be in that shower with her.

"I have no car," I said again, louder. "You drove me here, remember?"

Her silhouette shifted, and I got a perfect profile of her breasts as she tilted her head back and began rinsing her hair. Probably hit that pose on purpose. "Take mine," she said without skipping a beat.

"What will you drive?" I asked.

"I'll be fine. Just take my car. Keys are on the dresser."

"Okay," I replied.

I stayed fixed in my spot for a beat. Was I hoping for a friendly goodbye? I watched her silhouette continue doing its thing as though I was never there, as though I'd never been here.

I shut the door softly, grabbed her keys on the dresser, and left.

12

I hit up a drive-thru on the way home and gave a big middle finger to my waistline by getting a double-bacon cheeseburger and large fries. If a man ever had the justification for comfort food, I was him.

Angela's car was nice. New-car smell and all. It prevented me from cracking my burger for fear of dripping anything. Didn't even touch a fry, which, as we all know, is damn near impossible.

I decided to snoop a bit instead. Nothing major, just a peek in the glove compartment here, a yank on a visor there. I don't know what I'd thought I'd find—like I mentioned, the car smelled as though it left the dealer yesterday.

I'll call you when I need you, she'd said, right after we fornicated for hours like two sex addicts on a conjugal. Talk about a cryptic kick in the nuts. Where did that leave me? I had left this afternoon with the intention of finding answers. And I got them. And they sucked.

And now there were *more* questions.

I'll call you when I need you , she'd said.

Need me for what?

(*You know what, stupid.*)

Do I?

(*It won't be for more pussy, that's for sure.*)

So then what do I do?

I said it aloud. "So then what do I do?"

I didn't have to work until tomorrow. But who knew when she'd call? I may end up sitting at home with my thumb up my butt for days, waiting to hear from her.

Eat and sleep. I needed to eat—the smell of the fries was becoming maddening—and I needed to sleep. Although I had slept late today, I did not sleep as many hours as I would have liked (not to mention I was spent from sex), and I was notorious for sleeping when things were at their worst. Sleep was a pleasant escape to that uninhibited world I so endlessly pursued. I even welcomed nightmares and outlandish dreams because they would force me to *act* and *feel* on the spot as opposed to endlessly ruminating about what may be. No fish-bowl glasses of the world; no numb-wetsuit attire. You were there, in it, reacting without thought. Living for the now. Being in the now.

(*Ahh…such seemingly unattainable qualities, now being given to you like a gift that's ticking.*)

"No," I said to myself. "No, it's all wrong…not like this."

(*But it is like this. Sorry—no refunds.*)

Nope. This is all wrong. You don't know shit. Shut the fuck up.

(*I'm your fucking conscience, douche bag. I know a thing or two about you.*)

Yeah, and you've done a bang-up job so far; I'm the epitome of stability.

(*Hard for me to speak when I'm being constantly drowned in whiskey and cast off to some fantasy world pussies like you conveniently create.*)

Fantasy world? What the hell are you talking about?

(*Oh, you know…that safe little place you visit when fantasizing about how dark and disturbed you are? What you're capable of? Nothing but an armchair quarterback if you ask me. Except it looks like you might actually be thrown into the game pretty soon, yeah? See what you're really made of? What will we call Fantasy World after that?*)

You're fucking nuts.

(*Need I point out that you're talking about yourself?*)

Fuck you. I need to sleep.

(*I agree—my flight to Fantasy World is leaving soon anyway. Maybe I'll be back sooner than you think.*)

Take your time.

So sleep it was—after food of course. It was either that or get drunk, and as badly as I wanted to drink, I knew well enough to stay sober in case Angela called tonight.

(*Admirable—perhaps my flight will be delayed*)

Perhaps a 600 pound silverback will sodomize you while you wait and see.

(*Again—talking about yourself*)

Fuck off.

PART FOUR

PAUL

13

My food was gone in minutes. The double bacon cheeseburger, four bites tops. After that, I decided on a little TV to help with digestion before voluntarily slipping into a coma.

Pele wandered in as I was channel-surfing. He meowed as he always did when first entering a room. Cat-speak for: *I'm here; the party can start, bitches.*

I patted the sofa and he hopped up. I patted my stomach and he climbed on. In less than a minute he was curled up on my belly, purring louder than some men snore. I scratched his head and he purred even louder.

"Not a care in the world," I said to him. "Lucky bugger."

I drifted in and out over the next couple of hours, periodically waking for only a few seconds when the pitch in the television changed. When my cell rang, I woke for good—mainly because it made me jump; which made Pele jump; which resulted in him using my nuts as a springboard.

Doubled over and cursing my cat, I picked up my cell and checked the caller ID.

Paul.

I flipped open my phone. "What's up, man?"

"How's it going, brother?"

Paul was undoubtedly my best friend. Actually, my only friend. *True* friend. I had drinking buddies, but they were just that. Of course I drank with Paul, but we would still be inseparable if we gave up booze and stuck to lattes.

"You wouldn't believe me if I told you," I said.

"Why? What's wrong?"

I loved Paul, always told him everything. Things I was even afraid to tell my therapist.

So I decided to tell him nothing.

I had no idea what Angela was really capable of, where this whole fucked-up craziness may lead, and I didn't want Paul involved in any way, shape, or form. Just *knowing* may be too much at this point, and putting him at risk was simply not an option.

"Nothing," I replied. "Just a shit day."

"Nothing a few cocktails can't fix."

Christ was he right.

"I gotta work tomorrow," I said.

"I don't want to stay out late. Come on, let's go to Mick's and have a few drinks like gentlemen."

He was being very persuasive. It's easy to deprive yourself from a night of drinking when there was no offer on the table, but the thought of missing out on a good time with an eager friend bordered on the absurd. Still, we continued the dance, both of us knowing I would eventually cave.

"I'd wanna be home pretty early," I said, praying he wouldn't ask why.

"Why?"

It made me sick, but I lied to him—sort of.

"Well, I have to work…"

"And…?" he cooed, knowing me too well, the fucker.

"And I'm kind of waiting for a call."

"From who?"

"Some girl at work."

Kinda true, right?

"*Aaaahhhh…*" he said. "Do I know her?"

I needed to bury this thing now.

"Nah—it's not like that, man," I said, as blasé as possible. "It's one of my managers. It's a work thing."

"You are aware of the primary purpose behind a cellular phone, yes?"

"If it's noisy in the bar I might miss the call."

"So put it on vibrate, let it tickle your balls. Win, win."

I laughed.

He said: "You want me to pick you up?"

"No, that's alright. I'll meet you there. Give me an hour to get showered and shaved." This seemed most logical to me; if Angela *did* call tonight, I would need to be able to move about freely without having to rely on Paul for transportation.

"Alright," he said. "Do a good job though—I hear it's like 70's porn down there."

"Your sister's a liar."

We laughed and hung up. I took my time getting ready. Checked my cell several times to ensure it was completely charged. I was not sure whether or not Angela even had my cell phone number, but something told me she would find me when she needed to. I also noticed—peeking out my bedroom window—that her car was no longer in the parking lot where I'd left it.

14

I pulled into the parking lot of Mick's Tavern and spotted Paul's gray Jetta with the Yankees bumper sticker already in attendance. I bet myself he would already be sidled up to the bar, beer in one hand, pretty girl in the other.

The moment I entered, I collected on my bet. Ironically, Paul was a people person, the complete opposite of me. He was so utterly likeable that even a complete xenophobe (fear of strangers; I looked it up) would not hesitate to jump into his lap upon meeting him for the first time. I envied him at times, not so much for who he was, but for his outlook on life—the glass wasn't just half-full for my friend, it was half-full with liquid gold. How we became as close as we did was a paradox I never bothered dissecting. Why would I? Paul was like a windfall from a relative you never knew. You don't dig too deep into that kind of thing, you just enjoy it.

"What's up, my brother?" Paul said as I approached, getting off his stool to give me a hug.

I returned his hug and added a firm couple of pats on his back. It was good to see my friend.

The girl he'd been chatting with smiled and said to him, "It was nice meeting you. Maybe I'll see you later?"

Paul smiled back. "Definitely."

Both of us looked at her ass as she walked away.

I said: "I smell or something?"

"She's shy," he said. "And yes, you do."

The bartender appeared. Tall, good-looking dude, built like a superhero. Probably took home a different girl every night.

"What can I get you, man?" he asked me.

"Shot of Beam and a lager."

He nodded and left.

"Coming strong out of the gates," Paul said. "Thought you had to work tomorrow."

"Let's worry about that tomorrow."

The bartender brought my drinks. I pulled out my debit card and handed it to him.

"Wanna keep this open?" he asked.

I pounded the shot then took a heavy pull on my lager. "Yeah—" I pointed to my empty shot glass. "—and an encore on that please."

The bartender nodded, spun, plucked the Beam bottle from the shelf, spun back, filled my shot glass, then spun back again and replaced the bottle on the shelf.

I threw back my second shot and took another swig of my beer.

"Dude, pace yourself," Paul said. "What about that phone call from your manager? You wanna talk to her hammered?"

(*Yeah, Calvin—what happened to staying sober in case Angela called tonight? Guess my flight to Fantasy World will be right on schedule—that is if I don't drown first.*)

I squeezed Paul's shoulder. "I'll be fine, man. Just taking the edge off."

(*So sad. You just can't help yourself, can you? How does the saying go? One drink is too many; a hundred is never enough?*)

"Day was that bad, huh?" he asked.

I nodded. "Could have been better."

"Anything you wanna talk about?"

I raised my beer to his. "Nah—I'm good."

He raised his beer and we clinked glasses.

"You sure?" he said.

I shook my head with conviction. "I'm good."

* * *

A few cocktails later and I was greeted by my old friend Mr. Buzz. Paul had his back to me, busy chatting up the girl he'd met earlier. I had a feeling I was going to be without conversation for a few minutes, so I went and ordered myself another round, intentionally skipping Paul so as not to disturb him. Don't get me wrong; I knew Paul would eventually introduce me to his new friend, but I thought it best to leave him be for now.

The fact that I knew Paul would definitely introduce me to the girl was probably one of my favorite qualities in his character. There was no doubt the man loved women, but he also loved his friends, and his friends always came before pussy. So many friends claim unbridled loyalty, but the moment a pair of tits bounced in their face you were a stranger, a threat to Mission: Laid.

Not Paul. Not ever. The man could be in bed with Salma Hayek, I could bang on his door, tell him I needed help, and he would instantly pull out (probably apologize to Salma) and come to my aid.

"Calvin, have you met Stacy?" he inevitably asked me, knowing very well I hadn't.

I smiled and shook her hand with a polite grip. "Very nice to meet you, Stacy." Then, looking at Paul, but loud enough for Stacy to hear: "She's beautiful."

Paul splayed his hands with a pleasant face that read coincidence. "I was just telling her the same thing."

Transparent attempt at denying compliment in 3…2…

"Stop it," she said, gushing smile asking for seconds .

Paul went on, feeding her her seconds. Plenty of dessert too. She smiled, giggled, blushed, chortled, and every other type of fawning verb for the next five or so minutes as Paul did his thing, mercifully limiting my contribution; he knew I was only there in body, my mind elsewhere. Not an unusual thing for me, and something Paul was more than familiar with. Many times he was able to hook me before I drifted too far, reel me back into a better place. It was his gift; something no one else had been able to do throughout all twenty-nine years of my life.

Except tonight my mind wasn't drifting towards the usual dark corners it had gone before. It was (justifiably, understandably, logically, no-shit-ably) pre-occupied with Angela. It all felt like the old tale about the monkey's paw. I had gotten my wish, gotten Angela, but at what cost? I had to kill someone.

(Yup.)

I killed someone.

(Yup.)

This is not a dream.

(Nope.)

What happened was real.

(Ladies and gentlemen, if you'll look out your window now, you should see the infamous Fantasy World just below. Fantasy World was first settled by vaginas too afraid to embrace the realities of the real world. Here, these vaginas cultivated a way of life capable of nurturing their pathetic little delusions of grandeur, far, far away from any actualities that may appear.)

Holy shit, I really fucking killed someone —

" CAL!"

I blinked. Both Paul and Stacy were staring at me. Apparently Paul had been trying to get my attention while I was lost.

"What?" I asked.

"You alright?"

No—I'm a killer.

"Yeah, I'm fine. I was just thinking."

Paul frowned, gave me that subtle look of his that asked if I was drifting again.

"Stacy's friends are going to meet her here in a few minutes," he said.

"We were thinking about getting a table in back. Sound good?"

I nodded. "Yeah, fine."

"Okay...Stacy, you mind grabbing a table? I wanna talk to Cal for a minute."

Stacy agreed, smiled, and then headed back. I knew what was coming next.

Paul inched towards me, spoke low and with a hand on my shoulder. "You sure you're alright, man?"

I can't tell him. I WON'T tell him.

"Yeah, I'm fine."

"You nervous about that call from your manager or something?"

I shook my head. "No, no, I'm fine; I swear. Just a little out of it, that's all."

He squeezed my shoulder. "You sure? You know you can tell me anything."

I needed to squash this. There was no way I was going to tell him anything. I just had to be sure I would not slip up in a drunken stupor.

(So stop drinking then.)

I needed some kind of guarantee.

(STOP DRINKING.)

So I hurt myself.

After convincing Paul everything was fine, I excused myself to the bathroom, near-empty pint of lager in hand. I found an empty stall and locked myself in. I gulped the remainder of my beer and flushed the john, the industrial-strength noise of the flush the exact cover I was looking for while I quickly smashed the pint glass on the rim of the toilet. What remained in my hand was the dense circular base of the glass—razor shards like flat icicles sticking out of that base.

I palmed the bottom of the broken glass, lifted my pant leg, and with one violent motion, jammed the base of the broken pint glass into my calf. The pain was bad, but not as bad as I thought it would be, the alcohol no doubt my Novocain.

I studied the result. The cuts were fairly deep; and it was bleeding a little more than I'd expected; but fortunately no glass had broken off and gotten lodged into my flesh.

I quickly gathered a large wad of toilet paper and pressed it to the wound. The toilet paper was red in less than a minute. I gathered another wad, and pressed again. Gathered another and pressed again.

This cycle repeated itself for several minutes until I was fairly confident the blood flow was not getting any worse, was in fact, getting better, perhaps beginning to congeal. I balled up a final wad and stuck it to the wound, blood holding the paper in its place. I rolled my pant leg down, grateful I was wearing jeans—khakis might have told the story if the cut started up again. I flushed the wads of bloodied tissue and any remaining glass shards. The thick base of the broken pint glass was too big to flush; it would have to go into the bathroom's trash can.

The wound had started to burn already, and this was good, but it also filled me with a strong sense of regret. It had been years since I had cut myself. It was a practice I used to perform in an attempt to try and feel, similar, I suppose, to the way a neglected child will misbehave in order to receive punishment—bad attention preferable to *no* attention. In my case, feeling pain was better than feeling nothing at all. It is a practice that may seem ludicrous to some, but in the spirals of depression, it can be as enticing as a swimming pool during a scorcher.

I'd gone years without cutting, and tonight I'd fallen off the wounding-wagon. But I was absolute in my reasoning. This evening's cut was not for lack of feeling; it was a reminder. I would undoubtedly feel this wound on my calf for the remainder of the night. And no matter how drunk I got, the wound would remind me that I could not say anything to Paul about the mess I was in. I was doing this for him.

(*So thoughtful. If you really cared, you'd just stop drinking. What if one of Angela's freaks is waiting for you when Paul inevitably drives you home?*)

I'll call a cab.

(*Weak—you know he won't let you do that.*)

Then I'll drive drunk; I don't give a shit.

(*Right—he won't let you spend money on a cab, but he's going to let you drive wasted? Try again, dumb ass.*)

Why are you always here now? You were never this fucking annoying before.

(*You never killed a guy before. Never agreed to star in films that make snuff look like Disney.*)

You don't know that for sure. You don't know that's what I'm supposed to do.

(*Sure I do. It's all been spelled out for you, dummy. A child could read it.*)

Why don't you just fuck off? Just fuck off .

(*Why not go drink some more? Try and drown me for good?*)

Good idea.

(*That was a test, you weak, weak man.*)

I don't care. Go back to your Fantasy World.

(*I wonder how long that world will be there, quarterback? Perhaps it won't be long before you're in the game and my flight becomes grounded indefinitely.*)

Fuck you. Go back.

(*So you can keep drinking?*)

Damn right. Go back to your stupid little world and prepare for a tsunami, bitch.

I tossed the broken glass into the trash and shoved open the door. I spotted Paul and Stacy and two new girls at a table towards the back of the bar. They were already tucked in and emptying their drinks. I headed towards them.

"Cal, this is Karen and Julie," Paul said, gesturing to the new girls. "And of course you already met Stacy."

I nodded my hellos, my calf burning.

"Are you gonna sit down?" Paul asked.

I nodded and took a seat near Karen and Julie. Paul had obviously made his choice with Stacy; she was practically in his lap.

I took in both Karen and Julie's appearance with casual glances east and west. They were both attractive. Julie was blonde, like Stacy, and Karen a red head, though I don't think it was a natural red. As far as I could tell, both ladies seemed to have nice figures. Karen looked as if she had fake tits: way too big and perky and close to the neck for someone as slim as she was. Some guys went nuts over implants; some guys hated them. I didn't really care either way. As the old saying goes: if you can touch them, they're real.

"So what do you do?" Julie asked.

"I'm a massage therapist," I replied with a little trepidation. Even after six years I was still wary of the responses I received after telling people what I did for a living.

"Really? Do you massage *men* too?" she asked, her tone proving my trepidations valid.

"Of course," I said. "I make most of my money on men. Word of mouth, ya know? Pun intended?" I mimed sucking a dick.

She studied me for a tick, unsure whether I was lying or just being a dick. 'Twas indeed both.

"You do not!" she finally blurted with all the grace of a belch.

My calf *and* my head now hurt. I needed a drink and I needed for this girl to stop talking. I decided to address Karen.

"You having fun over there?" I asked.

Her attention had been fixed elsewhere while her obnoxious friend was taking up my time. I prayed they didn't share the same demeanor.

"Yeah, I'm fine," she said with a nice smile.

"You're Karen, right?"

She nodded. "You're Calvin?"

"Yup."

I needed a decent opening before the awkward silence polluted the air.

"So how do you know Stacy?" seemed harmless enough.

"We all work together," she replied. "How do you guys know Stacy?"

I looked over at Paul, who now had his hand on Stacy's knee and was whispering something into her ear. She giggled and leaned in closer to him.

"We actually just met," I said with a little smile.

"Yeah—looks like it," she said with a little smile of her own.

I smiled again. Karen smiled again. Julie looked annoyed. I didn't give a shit.

"Do you guys need another drink?" I asked.

I prayed they would say yes. Please don't be the types who order one and then nurse the fucker for the remainder of the evening. Please be fun. I needed

(alcohol)

fun.

"Yeah, that'd be great. Thanks," Karen said.

They—along with Stacy and Paul—gave me their orders, and I headed off to the bar, eager.

15

It was seven or eight rounds later and I was drunk; my memory, even from minutes ago, was a sieve. As I was taking a piss, I tried to catch as much as possible before it drained away (my memory, not my piss).

I was fairly certain that Karen and I had become friendlier. And there was little doubt in my mind that Stacy was now ready to marry Paul. Did that Julie girl leave? Trying to focus on a particular incident was like trying to remember a film you saw as a kid.

I could still feel my calf, so I was quite certain I hadn't said anything to Paul. I couldn't have; Stacy had been with him ninety-five percent of the time.

How was everything else going? Was I being a fool? I'm pretty sure I was acting okay. A little affectionate and giddy, but nothing too bad. In the morning I would no doubt convince myself otherwise as my hangover-induced liturgy of doubt and insecurity would run endless laps in my head. Why couldn't I just be like the majority of people in here and embrace my drunkenness? Laugh at my own stupidity the next day? Have no fear or regret about my gaping lack of inhibition?

Why couldn't I be like that?

(*Because you're a depressed drunk. Fire and gas.*)

I thought I drowned you.

(*Still afloat.*)

I thought I wasn't depressed, I thought I was just a pussy.

(*Oh you're depressed—no question about that. You've been clinically depressed your whole life. Got dealt a bad hand.*)

But…?

(*But you're a pussy because you know you shouldn't drink, yet you do. You're a pussy because you convince yourself there isn't a line.*)

Line?

(*Between Fantasy World and here.*)

I don't follow.

(*Doesn't matter. It'll all be irrelevant soon, won't it?*)

"The fuck are you talking about?"

"*What?*"

I turned. Two urinals down, a big dude, bigger than me, was taking a piss and glaring my way.

"Sorry, man," I slurred. "Was thinking out loud."

He didn't respond. Just zipped up, washed his hands, and muttered something like "drunk fuck" before leaving.

* * *

I returned from the bathroom to find Paul alone at the table. The girls were gone.

"Where's Stacy?" I asked, although it probably came out more like, "Werztacy?"

"She left," he said. "They *all* left."

"*What?* Why?"

"You tell me." His reply was blunt, his face accusatory but calm.

"I don't know." I could feel my face getting hot with shame.

"You don't remember what you said?"

My face was on fire now. Ears burning. Hot flashes. Fewer words are so debilitating to the insecure drunk than: *Do you remember what you did?*

I started rambling like a guilty fool. "I wasn't being crude. She was hitting on me too. Was it her friend? She was a bitch. Fuck her. I didn't do anything."

Paul said: "What's all this shit about getting off on torturing people?"

I couldn't stop my mouth from falling open. I felt the blood leaving my face. "What are you talking about?" I managed.

"Karen said you asked her if she got off to people being tortured."

I swallowed. My Adam's apple felt huge, like a real apple. "I did?"

"Yeah," he said, eyes studying me. "It freaked her out. It freaked them *all* out. Why'd you ask her that, man?"

I tried to smile. "I don't know; I was probably just fucking around, man. You know me."

"Yeah, I do. But that's a pretty fucked-up thing to say—even for you. What aren't you telling me?"

"Nothing, brother, I swear. I just…I fucked up I guess. I'm sorry. I didn't mean to ruin your chances with Stacy."

"Forget her, man. I can meet a Stacy anytime. What I'm worried about is you. You've been off all night."

I reached down and squeezed the wound on my calf until I could no longer stand it. I played it off as though I was fixing my sock.

"I'm fine, man," I said, standing upright, swaying. "Really, I am. I swear. I have no idea why I said that shit."

Paul got up from the table, studied me some more. He didn't look entirely convinced.

I grabbed his shoulder, squeezed it, tried another smile. "Look, I'm hammered, okay? I just…I just need to go home, that's all."

"I'll drive you," he said. "You can leave your car here and get it later."

This seemed like a great plan—until I remembered work.

"I can't do that; I've got work tomorrow."

"Worry about that tomorrow," he said, allowing himself a little smirk for throwing my earlier words back in my face.

I shoved him and told him to fuck off. He laughed and it was like music. I let out a long sigh.

"So your boss never called you tonight?" he asked as we headed for the exit.

"No," I said. "Guess she'll call tomorrow."

16

What the hell is that? The Bee Gees? Why do I hear the Bee Gees? Okay…the fog is clearing, and…I'm in bed. *My* bed. Hung-over. The Bee Gees are playing on my clock radio. Please make it stop. I loved *Saturday Night Fever* and all, but fuck me, please make it stop.

A good slap on the snooze takes care of things. Back to sleep.

Sonny and Cher? Slap.

John Denver? What fucking station did I leave this on? Slap.

Huh? An *actual* alarm now? No more music? How did that happen? Slap. Slap. Slap. Slap! Slap! *Slap!! Slap!!!* What the fuck? Why won't it shut— ? *ohhhh….shit…*

I flicked open my cell, tried to sound sick. "Hello?"

"Calvin? It's Margaret. Your client's here. Where are *you* ?"

"Oh geez, Margaret, I'm so sorry. I've been up sick all night. I must have slept right through my alarm."

Sounded good, but what if someone at work saw me out last night? Did I see anyone from work at the bar? Think. No—I'm fairly sure I didn't. Doesn't mean someone didn't see *me* though. Shit.

"Well what do you want me to do?" Margaret asked, not even trying to hide her contempt.

"Tell them I'm very sick and very sorry, and I will gladly work on them for free if they reschedule."

"And your clients after that? Will you be alright in an hour?"

"No, Margaret, I don't think I will be miraculously healed in the span of an hour. Would you please call and tell them the same thing?"

She huffed then agreed. I hung up, and was back to sleep in less than a minute.

* * *

No alarm this time, just the incessant nagging of an alpha feline. *Enough of this sleeping shit; give me some attention* his headbutts into my shoulder said.

"Alright!"

I sat up in bed. Pele made a beeline for my face, rubbing his jowls against my chin, letting me know that he did indeed care for me, despite the fact that I was under the absurd illusion I was his master.

As I lay there and allowed him to finish patronizing me, I began to try and piece together the previous night's events. Some of it was a blur and some of it was clear. I'm sure I was hammered; the grenades going off in my head confirmed that. I'm also sure Paul and I had chatted up some ladies and...

Oh shit.

My face and ears started to burn as I remembered what I'd said to one of those ladies. The one I was getting friendly with. Paul knew too. Did I tell Paul anything about Angela? About the mess I was in? I don't think I did. Did I? God, I'm a fucking idiot.

I kicked the covers off and swung my legs over the side of the bed. As my one leg flopped against the rim of the mattress it felt like someone had touched a lit match to my calf. I grimaced, looked down and saw the wound I'd inflicted on myself.

I then remembered everything.

The images were hazy, but the content was all there. I *had* managed to keep everything from Paul. All the crazy shit that was said to the girl (and she was a mere blur and a nice smell at this point) could easily be written off as stupid, drunken behavior. God knows he was used to that. I breathed a very temporary sigh of relief.

* * *

An hour later, Pele was fed, and I had showered and attended to my calf. It was 1:30 in the afternoon, and since I had called out sick for work and my car was still in the parking lot of the bar, I was officially stranded. Good old suburbia. No car; you're fucked.

I wondered when I would be hearing from Angela. She had spared me last night, but the more I thought about it, I suppose she really didn't. She was there, in my head the whole time—my wounded calf and macabre gift of the gab towards the fairer sex was proof enough of that. And then there was my conscience. Lately the fucker just wouldn't shut up. The excessive drinking and whatnot I can understand, but all this crazy talk about Fantasy World...I didn't get it.

How is that possible? My conscience is me. I'M talking about Fantasy World. Why can't I understand my own thoughts?

(Denial.)

And like a cock-blocker when you're with a honey, he's there.

(You're too kind.)

How is it possible that I'm in denial about something I don't even understand?

(You understand—being in denial is just an attempt at burying your comprehension. Some might call it suppression.)

I know what suppression is, fuck stick. But how can I suppress something I can't comprehend?

(Same way a bad memory from childhood can be suppressed and forgotten.)

I just said I know what suppression means. I'm not talking about trying to forget when Father O'Malley made me touch his thing; I'm asking how I can suppress something I don't understand. All your stupid metaphors about football, and being in the game, and flights to Fantasy World...

(A priest made you touch his dick? I don't remember that.)

Because it didn't happen, stupid. I was using it as an example.

(I'm not going to explain anything to you. I won't have to.)

Why?

(Because it will all happen soon enough. Even a drunken fool in denial will be able to figure it out when the time comes.)

I won't. I won't be able to. Just tell me now.

(So you admit you're a drunken fool?)

Yes, yes—now tell me.

(Nope.)

Motherfucker.

(It's all right there in front of you, Calvin. You're not an idiot.)

You just called me a fool.

(I called you a drunken fool. You're a fool when you drink.)

If I stop drinking, will you explain it to me?

(I won't have to. If you stop drinking, your clarity will go through the roof. But you won't stop drinking.)

Yes I will.

(You'll forgive me if I don't hold my breath.)

I wasn't about to give myself the satisfaction of telling myself to fuck off again, so instead I focused on Paul. I wanted to call him. I knew he was disappointed with my conduct last night, and I knew that he had no doubt forgiven me, but it was essential I let him know all the same that I was truly sorry for my actions, and that he could rest easy in regards to my strange behavior.

I got his voice mail and hoped he wasn't screening my call. He did that when I was being weird.

"Hey, buddy, it's me. I ended up banging out of work today—surprise, surprise. I just wanted to apologize for last night. I don't know what the hell I was thinking. I guess I was just in one hell of a weird mood. Anyway, thanks for driving me home, I appreciate it. Uh...I guess that's it. Just wanted to call and apologize. Talk to you soon, bro."

Hopefully he'll get that message and laugh it off, and if I knew him, he would.

(*Will he? You've always been a little weird, but last night was something new.*)

He will.

(*We'll see.*)

I had the rest of the day ahead of me now—with no car. No car and a hangover that could bring Keith Richards to his knees. Back to bed? Nah, I wouldn't sleep. Watch a movie? Maybe. Eat? I had no food in the house, and no car to get it.

Delivery it was.

I rummaged through my kitchen drawers until a disheveled menu appeared. Wong Garden. Damn good Chinese food. They would do nicely.

After phoning in an order large enough to ensure a breakfast of leftovers, I retired to my den to wait. I tried TV first, found a decent news story which boasted recent developments in some crazy psycho shit that went down in western PA a few years back, gave up on that, and popped *The Omen* into my DVD player. Content, I sprawled out on the sofa where I was soon joined by Pele.

"Hey, brother," I said.

He squinted at me (I read that's how cats smile) and then proceeded to get comfortable on my lap, kneading my stomach incessantly before curling into a contented ball of black fur. I scratched his head and felt his body hum. I smiled. Nothing more soothing than a cat's purr.

"I love you, buddy," I said, scratching his head a bit more. His purring grew louder as if reciprocating and I began to wonder if I had ever cared for a person this much. My family, you ask? I'll get to them later. Right now I was wondering how someone could love an animal more than a person. Unconditional love I suppose. They are trustworthy. No hidden agendas. A brutal honesty about them that you will never find in people.

I loved all animals. Cats especially. Whenever I would tell people about my affinity for cats, haters almost always labeled them mean or sinister; men wouldn't hesitate to call me a fag. " *What kind of single guy has cats???* "

I used to argue with such clowns, but eventually found it as productive as debating religion or politics. In my opinion, cats are the coolest fucking animals on earth (assuming they haven't conquered other planets yet, which is very likely). I loved cats for the very reason many hated them: their independence. I admired it, respected it. You had to *work* for a cat's love. And once you got it, it was the greatest gift ever.

I gave Pele a scratch under the chin this time. He purred like a chainsaw.

* * *

It was right around the time when Gregory Peck was talking to the crazy priest in the park when the doorbell rang. The usual cheap metallic *clink! clunk!* now sounded like an angel thrumming a harp. Food.

I hurried to my front door and looked out the peep hole. No one was there.

"Hello?" I called through the door.

There was a pause. And then: "You have a takeout order?"

I peeked through the hole again. Still nothing.

"Yeah," I said. "Where are you? Stand in front of the door so I can see you, please."

Another pause.

"Take out order for Calvin?"

"Yes, that's right. *Please stand in front of the door.*"

I might live in the suburbs, but I wasn't about to open my door to whatever was behind curtain number one, *especially* given recent events. Besides, it always seemed like the *really* fucked-up crimes occurred in the 'burbs—a fine line between mundane and insane, I suppose.

"You want fucky, fucky?" the muffled voice said.

"*What?*" I jerked the door open.

Angela swung into view, giggling, my Chinese food in her hands. "Me rove you rong time," she said.

"Wow, that wasn't racist at all."

She rolled her eyes, but a little smirk remained.

"What are you doing?" I said.

"I'm delivering your food."

"How did you...?"

"Does it matter? I've got what you want."

I took the bag of food from her, dumbfounded, mumbled a thanks.

"What about my tip?" she asked.

I said nothing, still dumbfounded. She placed her hand on my chest and pushed me back into my apartment, took the food from my hands and set it on the coffee table. She spun me by the shoulders so that my back was to her. Hands around my waist, she stood on her toes and placed her lips to my ear.

"I haven't showered yet today," she whispered. "Can I use yours?"

I nodded.

She slid her hands from my waist to my cock. I was hard in seconds.

"Will you keep me company?" she asked.

"Yeah," I said, though I can't be truly sure—words were an obstacle in the way of blessed insertion.

She let go of me and took a few steps back. I turned and took her in. She was wearing this sexy little white sun dress that stopped just above the knee. All-white on Angela seemed wrong in theory, yet damn right in the real world. Perhaps it was the notion that it was so wrong that made it so right. Taboo 101.

The dress' color soon became irrelevant; in one swift motion Angela unhitched both shoulder straps and let it drop. No panties, no bra. All her.

I forgot the color of the dress.

She honed in on my shower like radar. Began walking away from me with that confident allure, hips banging left to right, tanned ass obeying those hips like a bell.

She stopped at the bathroom door, looked over her shoulder, licked her lips. "Are you coming?"

More prophetic words have never been spoken.

17

I was spent. With the dehydration factor from my hangover coupled with the hour of sex I'd just had, I was officially wrung dry. I wanted to bathe in Gatorade.

I watched Angela dress as I lay naked on my bed. She was pretty mechanical about it, saying nothing as she fixed herself up. She didn't even look my way.

"You want something to eat?" I asked her.

"No thanks," she responded, checking herself in the mirror.

There was an awkward silence, at least on my end there was; I'm not sure this woman was capable of feeling awkward.

"Okay, more Chinese for me," I said. "So what happens now?"

"Aren't you going to eat?" she asked.

"I meant what happens with us?"

She laughed. " *Us?* "

Well that was a humbling kick in the dick.

"No, not that…"

But it is *starting to become that, isn't it?*

(Christ, how delusional can you get?)

"I'm talking about the other thing," I said. "The…stuff you showed me before."

She continued fixing herself up in front of the mirror as she spoke. "I told you I would get you when I was ready."

"Can you at least give me a clue as to what I can expect?"

She sighed, finally turned and faced me. "Okay, Mr. Worry…geez. I've got some things I need to take care of right now. In the meantime, you eat your food and get some rest. I'll be back for you later."

"Later? *When* later?"

" *Later.* "

I gave her a frustrated look. She ignored it and went back to the mirror.

"Well could you at least help me get back my car?" I asked.

"Where is it?"

"A bar."

She applied some lip gloss, smacked her lips, turned from the mirror and said, "We'll play it by ear. We're going to be pretty busy tonight."

She bent over me, kissed me, and then bit down hard on my lower lip. I jerked away and frowned, started sucking on my lip. The coppery taste of blood was instant.

She smirked and left.

THE BAR

"Not a vampire?" the bartender asks.

"Dude—not a fucking vampire."

The bartender holds up both hands and nods an apology. "Continue."

18

We're going to be pretty busy tonight, she'd said. What the hell did that mean? Busy doing what?

(Not each other. That's my guess.)

Yeah, okay. Then while we're at it, why does *she keep screwing my brains out? She's already got me by the balls with that damn tape.*

(You saying you don't like it?)

Hell no.

(Then sit back—or hop on—and enjoy it.)

But why do it?

(You mean does she like you?)

No.

(Yes.)

I threw on a pair of boxers and a faded *Stooges* tee, then headed into the kitchen to reheat my Chinese food. Pele emerged from wherever the hell he was hiding when Angela was here—odd for him; he usually demands attention from any and all—and began circling my ankles, hinting at a taste of that delicious-smelling stuff I was heating up in the microwave, please and thank you.

When the timer beeped, I dumped the contents of the white carton onto a plate, then bent and flicked a piece into Pele's bowl. He approached, sniffed, and then walked away.

"No, huh?" I said. "Just wanted to make sure I was still your slave?" I nudged him with my foot. He returned a swipe then disappeared.

I settled into my sofa and finished watching *The Omen* as I ate.

19

It was midnight when Angela reappeared at my door. I had been dozing on and off and answered the door still dressed in my boxers and *Stooges* tee.

Angela, however, was dressed in the type of camouflaged attire hunters wear—jacket, pants, even a cap. It was odd.

I looked her up and down. "What's with—?"

"*Hey, Moe!*" she squeaked, right before slapping my face.

I took a step back and rubbed my cheek. "What the hell?"

She gestured towards my tee. "I love *The Three Stooges.*"

I continued rubbing my cheek. "Maybe next time just tell me."

"You big pussy." Then, spotting something to her left: "Speaking of pussy."

Pele made an appearance. He sauntered towards my ankles, yet kept a cautious distance from Angela.

"I didn't know you had a cat," she said. "Why didn't I see him last time?"

"He was probably hiding. Cats can sense evil."

"Funny," she said, squatting down and holding a hand out to him. "What's his name?"

"Pele."

She glanced up at me. "Pele? Like the soccer player?"

"Yes and no."

She stopped trying to win Pele's affection and stood. "I don't get it."

"I named him after Jose 'Pele' Landi-Jons, my favorite fighter. Guy's a legend in the sport of MMA. So much so that he was nicknamed 'Pele' in Brazil—after the soccer player."

"MMA?"

"Mixed martial arts. Ever heard of the UFC?"

"Is that the stuff where they fight in the cage?"

"Yup."

"Huh." She began wandering around my apartment, stopped in front of my free-standing heavy bag, and started tapping her fist against it. "Well it looked more like soccer to *me* ."

"What did?"

"What you did to the guy outside the bar the other night. The guy I paid. You head-butted him then kicked him around like a soccer ball. Didn't look like any martial art I've ever seen."

"You watch too many movies. Street fights are ugly."

She kept tapping her fist on the bag. "So you used to be a fighter then?"

"Me? *No way* . I just train whenever I'm not too lazy or hung-over."

"Why *no way* ?"

"I don't have what it takes."

"You seem to handle yourself okay."

"I always hit first. No such thing as sportsmanship in a street fight. If a well-trained fighter got the jump on me, I'd be fucked."

"Alex got the jump on you. One of your hands was even tied. You came out okay."

"Your definition of okay must be vastly different than mine. And I'm guessing Alex wasn't trained. I also had to use a fucking lamp and a baseball bat to beat him."

"To *kill* him," she said with a smirk.

I pretended her comment had no impact, merely continued with: "Like I said; no rules in a street fight—lamp, bat, whatever I gotta do."

"Hmmm…" she hummed in thought, fist back to tapping my heavy bag. Her daze then snapped and she spun and faced me. "So you ready to go?"

"Go where?"

She did a sexy pirouette in her fatigues and said: "Hunting."

PART FIVE

FIRST GIG

20

I was wearing jeans and a grey sweatshirt as per Angela's request. Something plain; something that didn't stand out, she'd said. We were in her car, she was driving, and something told me we wouldn't be hunting animals. Of course this was fine by me; I could never hurt an animal. Unfortunately, that left an alternative prey I shuddered to consider.

"What's going on? You promised no more surprises," I said.

"Did I?"

"Angela, don't fuck around."

"So serious," she said.

I glared at her profile.

"I told you; we're going hunting," she said.

I looked out my window. The safety of the suburbs was now a good twenty or so miles behind us. Ahead, we were entering an area of the city I would hesitate to wander through in the morning. For every functional building passed, a graffitied square of brick and decay was its neighbor. The street lamps seemed to operate in a similar pattern: one lit, one dead, one lit…

"What the hell would we hunt around here? Rats?"

She didn't answer, just continued driving. I looked out my window again. The trash that littered the ground had changed. Candy wrappers, cigarette butts, and beer cans were now shopping carts, tires, and old appliances.

We drove on for another couple of minutes. Up until now, the presence of people had been pretty sparse, but as we approached the upcoming strip I noticed a greater congestion of men and women lining the curb. It was then that Angela banked left into an alley, away from onlookers. She stopped, and we sat idling.

"What are you doing?" I asked. "This…this is not smart. We're ducks here."

She leaned in close, spoke fast but concise. "We're going to pick someone up. I want you to tell her that I'm your girlfriend and that I said you could have a threesome for your birthday. If she sees me, she should have no problem getting into the car."

"We're picking up a *prostitute* ?"

Angela's reply was a quick shift into reverse and backing out of the alley onto the main strip again. She rolled up to a cluster of women, about four in total.

"Angela, answer my question," I said.

"Don't be difficult, Calvin." She slowed to a stop. "I'm doing you a favor by helping you with this one."

"Helping me with *what* ? What are—?"

She hit the horn, cutting me off. One of the four women approached. She stayed a cautious distance from the car, but close enough to bend forward and get a look through my window. In a different world she might have been pretty—her vocation looked as if it had tacked on a weathered ten to what I guessed was a nineteen or twenty year-old life. Still, she was by no means unattractive; I'd slept with lesser catches during past nights of shitfacedness.

I glanced over at Angela. Through clenched teeth she said: " *Do it.* "

I rolled the window down, tried to smile as I said hello.

"You want something, baby?" she asked.

My tongue felt huge and in the way. "My girlfriend and I were wondering if you wanted to hang out."

She bent further at the waist, looking past me to see who was driving.

"You cops?" she asked.

"No, no," I said quickly, trying to follow it with a friendly chuckle, only to have it sputter out like the nervous offerings of a man caught cheating at a card-table full of guns.

"What'd you have in mind?" she said.

I cleared my throat; it felt like the fucking Sahara. "It's my birthday…my girl told me I could have a threesome."

The girl looked past me again, studying Angela.

Angela leaned over my lap towards the open window, flashed a big smile. "Trust me, I'm not overly wild about the idea to begin with," she said. "But I promised him." She ended with a shrug and another smile.

"It's gonna cost," the prostitute said.

"Not a problem," Angela said.

I watched the prostitute's shoulders drop. Sold.

Angela hit the automatic locks for the back door. "Climb on in."

21

The drive was quiet. *I* certainly didn't say much. Even if Angela and I *were* a couple planning on having a threesome for my birthday, small talk with a prostitute was likely as uncomfortable for them as their trade itself.

She told us her name was Stephanie. A girl-next-door kind of name. I found that curious. Could it have actually been her real name? I can remember a night when a stripper slapped a friend of mine for daring to ask Candy or Cocoa or whatever she called herself her real name. My buddy had been just hammered enough to forget strip club etiquette. He'd insisted—sadly, like many men do—that this stripper actually liked him. He wanted to get to know the *real* her, find out her *real* name. A slap and a fuck you was his reply for bringing the real world inside those dark doors that parodied pride and coddled lust. And that was only a stripper. A prostitute? I imagine you'd get a knife in your balls for daring to dig. The real world had no place poking its nose around during work hours—and likely thereafter.

(*Look at you talking about* the real world *.*)

You don't know any more than I do, so shut up.

(*Don't I?*)

We're the same person.

(*And yet I've been having you scratching your head these past few days. How does that work I wonder?*)

Maybe I'm crazy.

(*Ah yes—some kind of dual personality thing; the last refuge for desperate writers in need of a twist.*)

I don't know what to do. I really do need help.

(*Sorry—doesn't work that way.*)

* * *

Angela's vast foyer. The three of us stood in a triangle. I was not aware of my expression, but knew it had to be more like that of a guy holding in a tidal wave of a piss than one about to bed down with two women.

Stephanie confirmed this when she said: "You look nervous. You nervous, sweetie?"

I think I smiled, think I nodded. Whatever I did, it was enough for Angela to get concerned and take matters into her own hands. She approached Stephanie, got in close, said, "He'll come around," and then began tracing her finger over Stephanie's lips. "I think we may need to give him something to get him going first."

They started to kiss. I watched Angela's hands slide down Stephanie's body, tracing her curves, cupping her ass, letting her fingers glide towards the front, Angela's lips moving from Stephanie's mouth to her neck, Stephanie arching her head back, seemingly enjoying it, moaning as Angela's hand slid upward, circling the erect nipple with her fingertips, Stephanie's moans graduating to longing exhales, Angela running her hand back down towards Stephanie's ass…and then a sudden jerking movement, Stephanie crying out, pushing off, frowning, furiously rubbing a spot on her ass, demanding to know what had just happened.

And Angela said nothing. Only stared back, waiting.

Stephanie's eyes rolled back, her body crumpling to the floor an instant later. Angela bent and checked her pulse. Satisfied, she then stood and looked at me. If my face appeared lost before, I couldn't even begin to imagine what it looked like now.

When Angela smirked and started twirling a small syringe between her fingers, I got it.

22

"You don't expect *me* to carry her upstairs do you?" Angela said.

I didn't think, only reacted.

(*Like watching a movie, isn't it?*)

Stephanie was relatively light in my arms, making the trek upstairs bearable. I reached the top of the landing and banked right towards the infamous room.

"No," Angela called out behind me, "we're not going in there."

I shifted Stephanie in my arms and looked over my shoulder. "Where then?"

"Left. Last room at the end of the hall."

I followed her directions and found the room. The door was closed. Several locks were beneath the handle. One was a padlock. Angela, who was following close behind, nudged me to one side and went to work on the locks with a ring of keys like something a security guard might carry.

Stephanie was starting to feel heavy. As Angela finished with the last lock, I wondered if putting Stephanie down would be worth having to go inside the room and see—

Nothing.

The room was the antithesis of everything else in the house—at least everything I had seen up until now. It looked like one of those white rooms they stuck crazies in. No furniture, no rugs, not even a window. Just white and more white.

"Put her down anywhere," Angela said. "She should be out for at least another hour."

I set Stephanie down in the middle of the room. Angela turned to leave.

"We're just gonna leave her here?" I asked.

"It's fine. Come on, I need to get you fitted."

"Fitted?"

* * *

We entered the room we fucked in the other night. Angela opened up a walk-in closet bigger than my apartment. She began sliding hangers and opening drawers. Each time, I got a brief glimpse of what hung on those hangers, what occupied those drawers.

"You want me to wear one of those ridiculous outfits," I said. "Like the freak who came at me with the bat."

"I take it you didn't approve of his fashion sense?"

I said nothing.

"Fine—you can play it conservative, but I *will* cover your face. I also suggest you change your clothes. You don't want to get them messy."

Messy.

She tossed me a pair of denim overalls like the kind farmers wear.

"Will those be okay, Mr. Versace?" she said.

I fanned the overalls out and held them up against my body. I flashed on the film *Motel Hell* with a chainsaw-wielding Rory Calhoun running around in overalls while wearing a severed pig's head.

Oh please don't make me wear a severed pig's head.

"Come over here and pick out a mask," she said.

I marveled at how blasé she was about the whole process, as if she was an employee showing me items in a department store.

(And you're just letting it happen…watching that movie.)

I approached the dresser drawer she had opened and looked inside. There were five masks all in a row. Two were all black with stitches and zippers all over the place, similar to the one the freak wore; one was a black hood similar to the executioner's hood I saw in one of her videos; one was a white ski mask that looked to be made out of leather; and the last one was, I shit you not, a plastic Elmer Fudd mask. I picked Elmer up.

"Anyone ever choose this one?" I asked.

She snatched it from me and placed it back in the drawer.

"Well what's it there for then?" I said.

"Are you going to choose or am I?"

I picked up the white leather ski mask.

"Perfect—that'll provide good contrast with her blood," she said, still as blasé as they come.

Her blood.

(Just watching that movie—popcorn and all.)

Angela opened another drawer on the dresser. She removed something and handed it to me. It was a box-cutter.

"A box-cutter? What am I opening?"

"Stephanie. I won't let you out until she's dead."

Her words were an ice blast. Or maybe it was the cavalier way she spoke them; the way she'd *been* speaking. Either way, it fucking sucked. Either way, I was fucked. Either way, it fucking sucked that I was fucked.

"Angela," I said, holding the box-cutter in front of her, "it'll take forever if I use this." I fingered the small thin blade. "This thing can't be more than two inches."

"That's the idea. The client doesn't want it to be quick."

"Jesus Christ."

Am I really going through with this?

(Disassociation.)

What?

(Like watching a movie about yourself. You might question character judgment throughout, and you might yell at the screen whenever that character does something stupid—very apt here—but in the end all you can really do is sit back and watch. Sorry, CHOOSE to watch.)

So what do I do?

(Well, wouldn't "living in the now"—as you so longingly aspire—be something you should finally man up and do? Give the film an alternate ending?)

Okay yeah, yeah. How though?

(I don't know. Maybe you need to get in the game for a little bit first. Get sacked a few times. This isn't a zero to sixty thing after all.)

You telling me to go through with this!?

(Weren't you going to anyway?)

No!

(Sure as hell seems like it so far. And you know what's saddest of all?)

What?

(Part of you is doing it for her.)

Well no shit.

(You know what I mean.)

Then I won't do it.

(Yes you will. It'll all be over before you even realize. Someone else has the remote.)

No.

(Why not? Drinking, street-fighting, romanticizing about how dark and enigmatic you are? It hasn't done shit your whole pathetic life. Why not get in the game and take a few REAL hits, hot shot? Maybe it'll finally man you the fuck up, allow you to make alternate endings for future films. Present you with a big red button to press so you can nuke Fantasy World into fucking orbit.)

Stop talking in metaphors!

"Still with me?" Angela asked.

I blinked and nodded. "You're going to film this I assume?"

"Of course."

"I didn't see any cameras. There were no cameras in the room."

"There are cameras. Here." She handed me her ring of keys along with a small tube of something. "Those are the keys and smelling salts. Get in there, wake her up, and then go to work. Don't fuck this up, Calvin; I've been good to you thus far."

"If you wanted to be good to me, you'd destroy the tape."

"If I destroyed that tape, I would never hear from you again. You might even end up growing a conscience and try to turn me in."

"I wouldn't turn you in."

"Be that as it *may*... " She took me by the shoulders, spun me around, and marched me out of the closet. "I'll be watching from in here," she said.

"Where?" I said, my head going all over the room, looking for I don't know what.

"The cameras feed into my TV. Stop stalling, Calvin."

"Tell me something," I said. "If I'm supposed to kill this girl, what's stopping me from just killing you?" I held up the box-cutter.

She smiled. "Nothing. You could do that I suppose. But the tape would still be out there wouldn't it? You'd have no way of knowing where it was, or how many copies I'd made. Jesus, Calvin, you act as though I'm an idiot.

"The bottom line is that you have two choices: you can do what I tell you to do, or you can take your chances with the tape."

I dropped my head and stared at the floor.

"Besides," she said, pressing her body against mine. "I don't think you want to leave. Who else is going to fuck you the way I do?"

"I've had plenty just as good as you," I said.

She gave a little smile, closed her eyes and nodded; indulging what we both knew was a lie.

I turned and headed down the hallway. Time to kill Stephanie.

23

I stood outside the room, the door still locked. In my hands were the keys, the smelling salts, and a white leather mask. In the pocket of my overalls was a box-cutter. On the other side of the door was an unconscious prostitute I was supposed to kill.

I did the locks quickly and without thought. Stuffed the ring of keys in my overalls.

The mask. I had to put it on before entering. There were cameras. I didn't see any, but Angela said they were there.

I pulled the mask over my head slowly. It was a snug fit, molding tight to my face. I had holes for my eyes, nose, and mouth. Dare I say it was comfortable as far as masks for this kind of thing go?

I opened the door and quickly stepped inside. I spun and shut the door behind me, my back to Stephanie. I couldn't look at her. Not yet. I just stared at the door, my breath erratic, heart thumping like a fist on my chest.

(You gonna do it?)

I patted the pocket of my overalls, felt the bulge of the box-cutter.

I can't do it.

(Angela will be upset.)

I don't care.

(Don't you?)

How did I get here? How did it get to this?

I turned around.

Stephanie was there, on her feet, facing me.

How——? was the only thought I managed before she kicked me in the nuts. I instantly doubled over in pain.

" *Fuck you!* " she screamed, and kicked me in the face with enough oomph behind it to drop me to a knee.

She backed up for another kick and I dove forward, catching her leg, driving her to the floor, me on top.

" *Fuck you fuck you fuck you!* " She wiggled and bucked with insane strength, arms flailing like studded whips, trying to hit, claw, and rake whatever they could. Catching and controlling those whips would be like snatching cobras. Fuck that.

I dug into my pocket and withdrew the box-cutter. Slid the blade out of its shaft, grabbed and pinned Stephanie by the throat with my left, raised the box-cutter overhead with my right.

She started to cry—the anger and rage turning to fear and defeat. She mumbled something, her sobbing making words incoherent. I held my frantic breath as best I could to listen. The only thing I got was "mom."

She was asking for her mother.

I took my hand off her throat, lowered the blade, and maneuvered off her torso. "I'm sorry," I said. "Jesus, I'm so, so sorry."

Stephanie suddenly rolled and lunged, attaching herself to me, biting, gouging, screeching… *tearing at my mask.*

Panic set in. I shook her off and snatched the box-cutter. I don't remember much in the way of detail after that. All I *can* say is that the client ended up getting what they wanted: it took forever to kill her.

THE BAR

"So you went through with it, huh?"

I drain my scotch, reach for the bottle and nearly knock it over. The bartender takes the Macallan and pours for me. I nod thanks and immediately sip.

"Yeah…I guess I did," I say, eyes on the floor.

"You didn't want to…"

I shake my head, eyes still on the floor.

"So why did you?"

I finally look up. I imagine my face is like an orphan's out of Dickens. "I don't know. It all happened so fucking fast. She was fighting like a wild animal, trying to rip off my mask—I couldn't have *two* tapes out there with my face on them."

"You said you do all that martial arts stuff. Why not just knock her out? Put her in some kind of hold and restrain her?"

Eyes back on the floor. "I don't know…like I said, it's kind of a blur. I didn't want to kill her. She just kept fighting though…no matter how many times I cut her, she kept fighting."

"Is that how you lost your ear? Is that why your face is all messed up? She do that to you when you were fighting?"

I shake my head. "No." I wave a hand across my battered face. "All this happened later."

"Do tell."

I glance up at him with only my eyes. I can tell he still thinks I'm full of shit. Assuredly even more so after my recent account with Stephanie.

And I still think that's just fine. Ironic though. When I first walked in here, the guy looked frightened, ready to call the police. Even when I threw hundred dollar bills in his face, assured him I would be a kitten on a stool, he still held that look.

He only started to relax when I began telling the truth.

24

I sat on the floor in a daze, Stephanie's body next to me. Her face and neck were a mangled mess, a good portion of that mess all over me. I thought of Angela's morbid comment about the white mask and blood, the contrast it would make. There were no mirrors in the room, but I'd wager Angela would be pleased.

I heard the locks begin to click and slide, the door opening.

"We're done," Angela said. "You can take your mask off now."

I looked at her. "How do I know you're not still filming?"

She raised an eyebrow. "Because I'm not wearing a mask—and I'm standing here in the room with you."

I ripped the mask off and flung it into the corner.

"So?" she said. "How was it?"

"Weren't you watching?"

"Yes," she said. "I want to hear it from you."

"Hear what?"

"How you feel."

"I feel like I need a drink."

"Come on…"

I got to my feet. "What do you want me to say?"

"Just tell me how you feel."

"I don't know."

"Excited?"

I said nothing.

"Scared?"

I said nothing.

" *Aroused* ?"

I glared at her.

"Come on, Calvin, say something."

"I feel like I just killed someone."

She shook her head as though disappointed in me. "No you don't."

"Whatever. Fuck you. I want a drink."

She eyed up my gory overalls. "Don't you think you should get cleaned up first?"

I splayed my arms, putting it all on display. "What for? This bother you?"

She rolled her eyes as if I had the audacity to match wits with her. "Bother me to look at? No. Bother me if you sit your bloody butt on my furniture? Yes."

I snorted. "Such are the pitfalls of your fucked-up trade, Angela. Deal with it."

She casually strolled towards Stephanie's body. "Well then you should at least move her first."

"Why? She's not going anywhere."

"We have to get rid of her, Calvin. Why not get it out of the way now so you can relax later?"

"So nice of you to take my feelings into consideration, but fuck that. Stephanie can wait."

Angela squatted next to Stephanie's body, examining the shredded meat that used to be her face. She seemed unfazed by my defiance, choosing a quiet indifference as her means to regain dominance. After a good minute or two—she continuing to inspect Stephanie's remains in silence as though I wasn't there; me standing behind her in bloody overalls, all but folding my arms and holding my breath like a kid—I eventually cracked.

"What did you mean by get rid of her?" I asked. "Get rid of her how?"

She stood upright, dusted herself off. "I have a place."

"What do you mean? What kind of a place?"

"So many questions. Just try and relax, Calvin."

"Yeah, well, I'd *like* to, but you're the one who's telling me I need to get rid of her body first."

Angela held up a hand and nodded, looking mildly annoyed as she placated me. "Alright, alright—I think maybe you do need a drink first."

"Fuckin' A." I turned and left the room.

25

My glass of scotch was half-empty by the time Angela entered her living room.

"Feel better?" she asked, motioning towards my drink.

"No—but after a few more I will." I drained the remainder in one gulp then poured myself a refill.

"You feel ready to talk yet?" she asked.

"I still don't know what you want me to say."

She stared at me.

"Okay," I began, "you wanna know how I feel, right? That's what you want? *How I feel*? Okay, here goes…" I took a sip of scotch, cleared my throat. "I feel conflicted. I feel conflicted because, well, let's see; I'm standing here in a mansion, drinking a glass of scotch that probably costs more than my rent, *with chunks of fucking flesh on me.*" I took another sip. "I feel conflicted because now I haven't just killed some freak in self-defense; now *I am* the freak. I've committed premeditated murder. Gave all those sickos you call clients something to jerk off to so your crazy ass can make a profit. And you know what?" I took another sip, let out a pathetic laugh. "Here's the sickest part. The part I simply *cannot* understand. There's a part of me—an exceptionally *fucked-up* part—that went through with this insanity just to get your approval. I mean for fuck's sake, most guys try roses and Hallmark cards; I gotta kill a whore with a fucking box-cutter."

I finished my drink, turned back to the bar, poured another. Angela slid up behind me. I didn't turn around.

"You don't have to be ashamed of your feelings for me," she said.

I kept my back to her. "Well, I am. If I wasn't so fucked in the head, I would have turned us both in by now."

"Don't say that. You know despite what you might think, I'm not using you for strictly financial purposes."

I snorted.

"It's true. I have no choice in what it is that I do." She placed her lips to my ear, whispered: "*So why not bring someone as sexy as you on board to make it all worthwhile?*"

I turned quickly and faced her. "What did you just say?"

"It's true, Calvin. I *do* like you."

"No, not that. What you said about not having a choice."

"What?"

"You just said that you did this kind of stuff because you had no choice."

"I think you misunderstood."

"No, no, you *just* said—"

" *Calvin* …I really think you misunderstood."

I groaned and turned my back to her again. "Fine. Whatever."

She leaned into my ear again. "Do you want to watch?"

"Watch what?"

"Your big debut."

I turned and glared at her, then took my drink to the sofa and stretched out.

"I'll take that as a no then?" she said.

"Take it any fucking way you want. In fact, if you really wanna take something, how about coming over here and taking my cock in your mouth while I finish my drink?"

"Excuse me?"

"Oh, I'm sorry, are you the only one who's allowed to initiate things? You wouldn't be using sex as a *tool* now would you, Angela? No, of course not. That would make you no different than that poor girl upstairs, wouldn't it?"

"Well you're just brimming with confidence. Maybe this *was* a good experience for you."

"Rattle off all the psychological bullshit you want; my dick is still dry."

We locked eyes. Another game of defiance. I was *not* going to lose this one.

"I'll tell you what," she said, "you go upstairs and bring Stephanie down so we can get rid of her, and then maybe later I'll make things worth your while."

I hurled my drink towards the stone fireplace, the fine crystal shattering into a mist. Angela flinched and I liked it.

"I'll tell *you* what," I said. "Why don't you shut up and come over here and do what the fuck I asked you to do."

She turned to leave, but I was on my feet and behind her in a blink. I wrapped my forearm around her neck and pulled her back towards the sofa, my other hand tearing at her clothes as she struggled to get free.

"We're all animals, remember? We don't ask; we just take."

My words prompted her into action, but I expected this and upped my own aggression. I had her pants around her ankles, had her bent over the arm of the sofa. I went to work with feverish intent, moving in and out of her like a piston. Her struggles fueled my desire, each protest making me thrust harder. I was giving it to her. Showing her that she did *not* pull all the strings. She may have my ass on tape, but by God I could inflict *some* sense of dominance couldn't I? Couldn't I? *Couldn't I... ?*

Why is she moaning like that? Is she enjoying this? She is! She is!!

I immediately pulled out.

" *What?* " she said, turning towards me, panting. "Why did you stop?"

I said nothing and backed away, the overalls around my ankles nearly tripping me.

"Why did you stop?" she asked again, still breathless. "That was amazing."

"Forget it," I mumbled, pulling my bloodied overalls back on. "I don't get you."

"Well, you're not the first man who's said that to me," she said as she began inching up her panties.

"Oh you're such a sexy fucking enigma aren't you? Give 'em a little taste and they'll kill for you right? You know what? I don't think you *are* any different than that whore upstairs."

"My face doesn't look like hamburger."

"Fuck you. Tell me what you meant earlier about having to do it."

"Oh we're back to that now, are we?"

"Tell me!"

She took a step back, held up both hands to try and soothe me. "Calvin, even if I *wanted* to tell you..."

So I *did* hear correctly.

"Tell me what? Come on, tell me what?"

"Can we just move on please?" she asked. "We need to move Stephanie."

"If I get rid of Stephanie will you talk to me?"

She walked towards me and placed both hands on my waist. I thought she was about to kiss me until she spoke.

"We've got a good thing going here, Calvin. It sounds to me like you're trying to complicate things."

"I'm not trying to complicate things. I've already done what you wanted me to do, right? All I was doing was reacting to something you said, that's all." I took hold of her hands on my hips. "Just tell me. Please?"

She did not pull away, but her face expressed something I'd never seen in her before. For the first time, Angela Thorne looked uncertain.

"Okay, okay," I said. "You know what? We'll let it go for now. What do you want me to do with Stephanie?"

She raised an eyebrow at me. No doubt she was shocked at how quickly I had let the subject drop, how quickly I had gone from rapist to counselor.

Truth be told, this was part of my plan. Trying to outfox someone as wily as Angela was like playing Xbox with your toes. I knew that any obvious attempt on my part would be fruitless, so I opted to play the waiting game. My hope was that in time, she would eventually slip up and divulge a little more information to me just as she'd done only moments ago. That little nugget of optimism was enough to keep me quiet and obedient—for now.

"I have a place where we can bring our subjects," she said.

"Our subjects?" I said. "You mean the people we torture and kill."

"The people *you* torture and kill."

"The people you *make* me torture and kill."

"It's an incinerator," she said. "There will be nothing left. No traces."

"What about the people who saw us pick her up? They could go to the police."

She laughed. "No cop would care. Occupational hazard."

I hoped she was right.

I asked. "You burn 'em?"

"Yup."

"Where is it?"

"I'm going to give you directions. You can put her in the trunk of my car and take her. Come straight back when you're done."

"A 'please' would be nice."

"Do I really have to say please?"

"No, but it helps when you treat me like a slave."

She gave my cock a stroke. "Pretty please?"

I pulled away as I felt myself getting hard. The powerful bitch had enough leverage over me. I felt like I'd won something earlier and I wasn't about to trade that in no matter how much I wanted to bend her over that couch and finish what I'd started.

"Thank you," I said. "Was that so hard?"

"It was getting there."

I ignored her wit. "Directions?"

She produced a folded sheet of paper and handed it to me. "Don't be stupid and run any lights or anything. You'll have a body in your trunk."

"Thanks for reminding me."

PART SIX

WHAT NUMBER AM *I*?

26

The location of the incinerator was close to the same unsavory neighborhood where we'd picked up Stephanie, and I was worried about being spotted by one of her "co-workers." I'd mentioned this to Angela again right before I left, and, like before, she merely laughed it off and reminded me about occupational hazards—no one would care if Stephanie went missing for a few days, let alone hours.

Still my nerves were all over the place. Never mind I was in a neighborhood that Robocop would avoid. Never mind I didn't have a clue where I was, or precisely where I was going in said neighborhood. I had a dead body in my trunk. A body I had killed.

(Sinking in, is it? Fantasy World must feel galaxies away right now.)

I'm not sure. I'm more worried about getting caught, I think.

(More than the fact that you brutally murdered someone?)

I murdered that freak…

(Stephanie was different, and you know it.)

No it wasn't…I didn't want to…I was going to let her go.

(But ya didn't.)

She attacked me after. I was defending myself.

(Please.)

I was.

(I'll give you the freak. But Stephanie? You didn't have to kill her.)

Why am I still numb? You promised if I got in the game, took a few hits…

(How the hell should I know? If you don't know, then I don't.)

What!? You know everything! Where are all your stupid fucking metaphors?

(Maybe you're still numb because of what Angela said earlier. Her words keep you numb until she decides to give you more.)

You think she's playing me?

(She's BEEN playing you. You even unknowingly admitted it to yourself earlier: you'd be quiet and obedient until she gave you more.)

That's different; I'm using a ploy.

(Different but the same.)

She doesn't have to fuck me. Why is she fucking me?
(Keeping the help happy?)
You saying she fucked all those freaks?
(You considered it before.)
That was a while ago. It's different now.
(Hahahahahahahahahahahahahahahahahahaha...)

I followed the last line of directions that had me turning into an alley off the main road, the street lamps behind me growing distant as I rolled on, my headlights soon becoming my only source of light in what began to feel like a tunnel.

The alley was predominantly bare as far as alleys go—a few battered trash cans; plastic bags and newspapers trying to fly. My speed (which couldn't have been more than 10 mph, if that) taken into consideration, the alley still seemed to go on forever. Perhaps I was lost, was down the wrong alley, hell, the wrong block.

I reached for the directions on the passenger seat, glanced at them for a tick, glanced back up, and then stomped the shit out of my brakes. A wall to what was a dead end seemed to materialize out of nowhere. I sat there, idling for a moment, heart racing, headlights shining on a stone wall covered with graffiti.

So what now? Did I wait? Would someone approach me like a drive-thru window? Ask me how many bodies I'd be dumping today, sir?

I waited another minute, car still idling, headlights still on, reading the graffiti I could understand.

(You're going to have to get out of the car.)

I took a deep breath, held it, switched off the ignition, and got out. A dim source of yellow light about ten yards east was my only beacon. I followed it until I came to a large metal garage door. Above the door jutted a solitary bulb encased in a wire cup, the source of light. No doubt this was my destination. I saw nothing else of significance. Either I was indeed lost, or this was it.

The garage door was huge and solitary, no adjoining doors on either side. The building that held the door did not look like a building, at least not in the traditional sense. It did not protrude from the wall, did not appear detached in any way. It looked as if someone decided to fasten a giant garage door into an endless wall of brick and stone.

I rapped my fist on the metal door, light at first, and then a bit harder. The echo that came back was louder than I wanted and made me look both ways. I was very alone. On another planet alone.

The door rattled and clanked from the other side. Someone was there. Another metallic clank, the sound of a bolt sliding, and the door started to slide upwards.

I saw dirty boots first. Then dirty jeans. Then a dirty sweater. Finally a dirty face. The guy looked like someone you'd see holding a cardboard sign on a street corner. His beard was a salt and pepper mess, more pepper than salt, though I think filth took more credit than genetics. Gun to my head I'd guess him in his forties, but his leather skin would have made a good argument for fifty-something. He spoke first, and when he did, I noticed his front teeth were gone.

"You droppin' something off?" he asked. Without his front teeth, *something* sounded like *sumfin* .

"I'm not sure," I said. "What do you know about it?"

I was paranoid and scared. For all I knew the guy could have been talking about a stolen car I'd brought him to chop. I needed him to be specific.

"The sexy lady sent ya," he said. "You're droppin' off another one, right?"

"Depends. What do you know about it?" I said again.

He looked annoyed. "I know that if you want somethin' gone, you give it to me."

This had to be it, and this had to be the guy. The odds that I was speaking to some random transient who happened to know a sexy lady who'd sent me to drop off "another one" were slim to none. So I went ahead and started getting it over with.

"Okay," I said. "How do we do this?"

Somehow I saw him smirk through that forest of a beard. I didn't like it.

"I'll open the garage," he said. "You back in. Then we deal with it inside."

I did as told. The dark interior of the building was vast and empty. It had a musty charcoal smell.

The two of us now standing in front of the trunk, the guy asked, "You gonna open it up?"

I popped the trunk but looked away. My periphery caught the guy reaching inside the trunk, fiddling with the body.

"Did a number on her, didn't ya?" he said.

I finally looked. The guy had pulled back the sheet covering Stephanie. Pulled it back and down her torso. Her face and neck were a gory mess, but her bare breasts were still relatively intact.

"Nice tits," the guy said. "You get a chance to tap it before you carved her up?"

I ignored him. My silence got me another smirk through that mangy beard.

"So what do we do with her?" I eventually said.

"I don't do shit," he said. "I provide the means, you do the extremes."

"Any chance you can elaborate?"

The guy chuckled, started walking deeper into the garage. "Pick her up and follow me."

I refused to look at Stephanie's (lack of) face as I lifted her out of the trunk and followed the guy deep inside the garage, all the way to the far end. He pointed to a hatch on the wall that looked like a big laundry chute. "Well go on, boy—slide her on down."

"Where's it go?" I asked.

"Incinerator."

"You sure?"

He smiled. "Yeah, boy. This ain't the first time I done this."

I shifted Stephanie's body in my arms and gestured towards the shoot with my chin. "Well can you open it for me?"

He scratched his beard as if thinking about it, as if it was one hell of a favor I was asking. Finally: "Sure thing, boy."

The guy jerked the hatch open. I instantly felt the heat from somewhere below.

"Jus' slide her on down the chute and that'll be that."

I did it quickly. Heard Stephanie's body clang and bang along the corridors of the chute as it tumbled down. There was a final thud, a sound like gears grinding, and then a blast of heat rocketing up the chute that hit me square in the face.

"Jesus!" I yelled, turning away from the chute and shuffling to a safe distance.

The guy laughed. "Almost like a dragon ain't it?"

I said nothing.

"Shame. Looked like a damn good piece of ass, that one. You get a chance to do her first?" he asked me again.

I began walking back towards the car. He followed.

"No, I suppose not," he said to my back. "You're a good lookin' fella. I reckon you're fuckin' the sexy lady who sends 'em here, yeah?"

I continued heading towards my car, doing my best to ignore him.

"Are ya? Are ya fuckin' the sexy lady? Yeah—I reckon you are. Every other fella she sends has had some of that."

I stopped suddenly. Turned and faced him. "What did you say?"

"'Bout what?"

"About other guys coming here."

He gave me that smirk again, and I envisioned snatching his beard and ripping the fucking thing off.

"Hell, boy—you think you're the only one she's fuckin'? She's always sending a new one my way. I reckon your number five this year. Maybe six. Hell, seven."

A mix of confusion and anger started churning in my gut. I certainly wasn't stupid enough to think that a woman like Angela had been saving herself for yours truly, but I *was* interested in knowing if she had blackmailed any other poor schmucks like me. And if so, where were they now?

(*You're also a little jealous.*)

No.

(*Yes.*)

"What do you know about it?" I asked.

"'Bout what?"

"The other guys she sends here."

The smirk again. "Why? You jealous, boy?"

Rip off the beard, shove it down his throat until he chokes, stomp on his head until purple shit comes out his ears...

"No, I'm not jealous," I said, probably sounding jealous. "I'm just curious as to where these other guys might be now."

He shrugged. "The hell should I know? I jus' do what I'm told and collect my pay at the end of each month."

"And how's that work?"

He smiled. "Friend of a friend of a friend."

I headed back to the car. He followed.

"Just enjoy that sweet pussy, boy. You keep asking too many questions and next time I might be talking to a *new* fella."

Shamefully, I contemplated his words. Would asking too many questions get me in trouble? Angela did say the freak I'd killed had been talking too much. My curiosity was split: half of me wanted to know what happened to the men before me, and the other half was portraying the jealous boyfriend who wanted details about former lovers. The first half was more than justifiable out of self-preservation. The second half was pathetic; it had no business in a fifty/fifty split with survival.

"Are we done here?" I said. "Can I go?"

He nodded once, spit, wiped his beard and said, " *Maybe* I'll see you again, boy."

I grunted and went to get in the car.

"You give that sweet pussy a kiss for me, alright?"

This last quip—while no different than any of his previous winners—changed that churning mix of confusion and anger in my gut into one hundred percent pure anger.

Was it because I felt like he was disrespecting Angela—

(*who cares???*)

—or was it because it felt like he was bullying me with secrets? I didn't know. I just knew that I wanted to kick-fuck the guy into a coma.

"You should watch your fucking mouth," I said, leaving the car, moving towards him.

He put his hands up in a pacifying gesture, yet continued with that condescending smirk. "Jesus, boy—you lettin' a woman control your mood and she ain't even here." He barked out a laugh. "You must be one pussy-whipped faggot!"

I dipped to my left and ripped a left hook into his liver. He crumbled to the ground instantly where he let out a sound like a punctured tire.

"What's wrong, man?" I said. "Legs give out on ya? Yeah—liver shots'll do that." I reached down towards his moaning, fetal body and got a good fistful of beard. "Here, let me help you up." I jerked, his head came off the ground a few inches, and then my fist came away with beard and skin and blood. The guy screamed. I smiled.

I tossed the hunk of beard and flesh back into his face, spit on him, then got into the car and drove off.

Felt good.

THE BAR

"What'd you do that for?" the bartender asks.

"Because the guy was a perverted scumbag. He got what he deserved," I say, gulping what's left in my glass as though the act of drinking fast and hard and excessive justified my point; proved that I'd been a man acting like a man. I think Hemingway might have understood.

"I'm not arguing about the guy; he sounded like an asshole, probably did deserve a few smacks…"

I nod emphatically, reach for the Macallan, but he grabs it first; probably afraid my drunken fingers will knock it over. He pours me a refill and continues:

" *But* ," he says. "Weren't you concerned as to what Angela might do? I mean, you're trying to get her to admit some big secret, right? What if what you did puts the kibosh on that chance?"

I sip my refill, shake my head. "At that moment? I didn't give a shit. Dirty old scumbag had gotten me so worked up; all I could think about was the other guys he kept referring to. Besides, I knew Angela wouldn't tell me anything when I got back—in fact, it would be a while before I got the *real* truth out of her. And fuck me, what I had to go through to get it."

"What? What'd you have to go through?" he asks, uncharacteristically eager for the moment.

I sip my drink and shake my head. "Not yet."

Besides, pal, if you think I'm full of shit now; just you wait. When I tell you, you'll ditch the boots and shovel and start looking for a fucking snorkel.

27

We were in Angela's living room. I was slumped on the sofa; she stood in front of me. I didn't look at her as we spoke.

"So talk to me," she said. "Tell me how it went."

"It went fine."

"I take it you met Manny?"

"I never got his name."

"Eccentric fella, isn't he?"

"To say the least."

There was a moment of pause.

"So it went okay then?"

"Stephanie's well-done if that's what you mean."

"Humor as a diversion," she said. "What are you hiding?"

"I'm not hiding anything. I'm fine."

"You don't sound fine." I could feel her stare. "You did dump her didn't you?"

"Yes, I dumped her." I finally looked up, trying to project some measure of confidence. "I also had quite the interesting chat with your buddy Manny."

"Did you?"

"Yes I did."

"What did you talk about?"

"Well let's see...first, he commented on your beauty—got a real gift of the gab that Manny does."

"He's harmless."

" *Then,* " I blurted, in case she intended to continue. "He happened to mention all of the men who were under your employment *before* me."

"Did he?"

"Yes, he did. It would appear that even decrepit men in seedy parts of the city know all about your sexual exploits and fetishes for all things macabre." I sat upright, gaining steam. "He told me there were guys before me. Guys just like me, doing what I was doing. Five, six, maybe even seven—he couldn't keep track. Five, six, maybe even seven guys you fucked like a porn star so they'd follow you around like puppies, doing whatever they're told. Or should I say, doing whatever they're told *or else*?" I splayed a hand. "You wanna tell me where those guys are now?"

She remained standing, never lost her composure. "Do you believe everything you hear, Calvin?"

"Why shouldn't I believe it? You told me yourself that you'd been following me. *Choosing* me. You told me that the freak I killed was getting sloppy and you had to get rid of him. Why shouldn't I believe that there were others before me; men in my exact predicament? How do I know that you're not planning to get rid of *me*? Should I feel safe because we're fucking? You were fucking all those other guys too!"

"Will you please calm down?" she said. "Please consider the source of all this information you're getting."

"That's just it, Angela. I *know* some of it is true. I *know* about the type of business you're in. I *know* about your fetishes. Call me crazy, but with absolute knowledge like that, it sure as hell makes the other stuff easy to swallow."

"You mean the stuff about the men before you?"

"Well, yeah," I said. "Where are they?"

"Why do you want to know? Are you jealous?"

"No—"

(*liar*)

"—I'd simply like to know if they're *alive* or not."

She rolled her eyes and took a long breath as though about to explain something for the umpteenth time.

"First, let's get something straight," she began. "I don't know where the heck Manny got his figures from. Believe it or not, there are people in this world that don't need to be blackmailed in order to work for me. Some work willingly if I pay them well. I'm sure those were the individuals Manny was referring to. It may have been five or six or seven, or even ten. It may have been two. They were my employees. They did what I told them to do, and I paid them for it.

"Second, the only one of those individuals that's dead is Alex, and that's because he was an idiot with a big mouth. As for the others, some are still working for me, and some are not. But as far as I know, they are all very much alive."

But did she fuck them?

I opened my mouth to ask, but she cut me off, reading me like the open book I was to her.

"And *third*, at the risk of giving you a king-sized ego, you are the only employee that I have ever slept with. My risqué behavior and questionable line of work does not make me a whore. I do what I do with you out of enjoyment, not necessity. Clear?"

Her words sunk in with minor prejudice; she had such a convincing way about her. And her comment about sleeping with me for pleasure did give my ego a stroke. But that feeling, while savored, was fleeting. It was unnerving to think I was so easily manipulated by her words when you considered the complexities of our fucked-up rapport.

I decided to try and play it indifferent.

"Whatever," I said, closing my eyes and rubbing my temples as though exhausted and with headache (which was true), nurturing the role.

"You don't have to believe me if you don't want to, Calvin. But it's all true. I have nothing to gain by lying to you."

I snorted at her remark. I wanted to make her work to convince me.

(*You know that won't happen.*)

"Well I'm glad that's settled," she said. "Feel better now?"

Her question seemed to carry a hint of condescension, and it made my recently dulled flame grow hot again. I figured this might be an ideal time to tell her about Manny's unfortunate meeting with my fist and revel in her reaction.

"Sure— *I* feel better," I said. "Don't know about your buddy Manny though."

"What do you mean? What about Manny?"

"Guy's got no manners," I said.

"So?"

"I taught him some."

I sounded stupid trying to talk in this Hollywood-tough-guy way. It just wasn't my style, and it felt ridiculous the moment it left my mouth.

"What are you saying, Calvin? Did you beat up Manny? Did you beat up an old man?"

"He fucking deserved it."

"You asshole."

I tried playing a different hand. "Oh I see; me beating someone's ass is only cool when you're the one setting it up?"

She shook her head, muttered "asshole" again.

"Well what's the big deal?" I said. "The guy's a fucking pervert. Just flash him your tits and everything'll be fine. He'll think it's his birthday."

She stared at me as though I'd pissed her bed.

"You know what?" I stood. "Fuck this. I dumped Stephanie like you asked; my job is done. Now if you'll excuse me, I'd like to go home, take a much-needed shower, get shitfaced, and then actually consider waking up for work in the morning. Would that be alright?"

Part of that was true. The other part was hoping she'd ask me to stay. I was exhausted, and a night of serious fornication seemed daunting, but the *offer* was all I really wanted.

"Well I guess you better be on your way then," she said. And there was no bait in her tone. Nothing I might be able to twist and lob back at her, starting the game. She'd made a flat statement. A goodbye and that was all. Actually, not even a goodbye. More of a: *you can go now* . It reminded of the first time we slept together, the cavalier way she'd spoken to me after while showering: *"You can go...I'll call you when I need you."*

"Yeah...see you around I guess," I said, a pathetic attempt at dangling my own bait.

She turned her back on me and walked away without another word, as elusive a catch as ever.

I left with my tail between my legs.

28

My alarm jerked me from a dead sleep. I'd been dreaming. About what, I don't know; everything broke apart the moment my eyes snapped open. The only thing that remained was a feeling of dread—liked I'd been drowning.

Pele was out cold at the foot of my bed. Only his ears twitched when I switched off the alarm and got up, the bastard. *Take my mice and my milk, but spare me my 23 hours of sleep!* I'm definitely coming back as a house cat in my next life. I figure the cleaning your butt with your tongue thing is a mere bagatelle when you consider the abundance of pros that existed.

A hot shower and many cups of coffee later and I began feeling as ready for work as I was ever going to be. I didn't get hammered last night as I'd planned, but I did strap on a hearty buzz. The kind of buzz that gave you mere headaches and a dry mouth, eventually cured by aspirin and coffee and Gatorade and McDonald's.

Shitfaced? You still treated it with all of the above, but you never won, only wounded the beast. Mere headaches were promoted to *"Please stop fucking talking"* aches. Dry mouth and bad breath was *"Who shit in my mouth while I was sleeping?"* mouth. And of course, all of their buddies—nausea, the sweats, the shits—were united in their promotion as *"Never again."*

And yet you do.

(You mean YOU do.)

I didn't last night.

(That's true; you stopped. No easy task once you've got a buzz.)

Thank you.

(Why do you think?)

Why what?

(Why did you stop?)

I was tired. I couldn't call out sick from work again.

(Admirable—although maybe there's more to it than that.)

I don't have time for your stupid puzzles wrapped in figurative language. I'm going to work.

29

Talk about fucking irony. I arrived at work to find my two clients had cancelled, but, saints be praised, someone else had booked in! Care to guess who that someone was? A week ago, I saw Angela's name on my schedule and all but came. Now, an explanation for her name filled me with the urgency of a piss.

"Margaret?" I said, the moment I reached the front desk.

Her eyes stayed on the computer screen, fingers clacking away on the keyboard as she answered me. "Mmmm…?"

"My client—when did she schedule her appointment?" I asked.

"About an hour ago."

"Did she say anything unusual?"

The clacking stopped; she looked up at me with only her eyes. "Unusual?"

"Yeah—did anything strike you as strange?"

She resumed clacking. "No—nothing strange. Two cancelled; she filled one of the spots. That okay?"

I don't know.

30

"Calvin, your client's here," one of the aestheticians said to me while I was brooding in the break room.

"Thanks." I steadied my breathing, put on a professional face, and headed up to the front of the spa.

She was there. She looked hot.

"Hi, Calvin—you ready for me?" Her tone was innocent and friendly.

"Sure am," I managed without cracking the pro face. "Come on back."

* * *

I shut the door behind us the instant we entered my room.

"You do happy endings, right?" she asked.

"What do you want?"

"A massage."

"Bullshit. What do you want?"

"Oh, Calvin—is the honeymoon over already?"

"You're not here for a fucking massage."

"It wouldn't be so unusual, would it? This is how we met."

"Things are different now."

"Because we've slept together?"

"You and your fucking games."

She rolled her eyes. "Relax."

"Did you make my previous clients cancel?" I asked.

"What? How the hell would I do that?"

"I don't know—how do you do *any* of the shit you do?"

"Should I be concerned about this paranoia? We're not going to start discussing JFK are we?"

"Yeah—have your fun…"

"Oh relax, Cal—"

"Stop telling me to relax!"

Angela winced and grimaced as if hearing a mic screech in a reverberant room. "Not sure you should be yelling like that in a place like this," she said.

"Stop playing fucking games then."

She nodded almost apologetically. "You're right—I know this isn't easy."

" *Do you?* I'm sorry, you see up until now I thought all you did was point a finger and say go. I had no idea you'd gotten those pretty little hands dirty before."

She looked annoyed now. "You don't know shit, Calvin."

"Whoop! Look out! Another hint from her *mysterious* past." I put a theatrical hand to my chin. "I wonder though; was it genuine? Or was it strategically placed to keep me intrigued? *Hmmm...* "

"Are you having fun?"

"Tell me what you meant about having to do it."

She sighed. "Back to that again."

"I never left it."

"Not now," she said.

"Why not? We've got an hour to kill."

"I'd rather have a massage."

"I'm not massaging you."

"Fine." She took a padded envelope from her bag and tossed it on the massage table.

"What's that?"

She didn't answer, only gestured towards it.

I picked up the envelope and opened it. Inside were plane tickets and folded papers. I read the tickets. "What's this? What's in San Francisco?"

"Your next assignment."

"You're making me do *more* ?"

She ignored my question, kept talking about the job. "We had a special-request project on phobias. The client wants a more distinct emphasis on the subject's feeling of dread before they die."

"Dread?"

"In simplest terms, this client gets off on watching people who are truly terrified."

"You're telling me past subjects weren't truly terrified?"

"Well, they were in pain, and they were in fear of dying, but they weren't terrified to the core—their deepest fears hadn't been exploited. That's what this client wants."

"I'm not following."

"What are *you* afraid of, Calvin? What *truly* terrifies you?"

"You think I'm gonna tell *you* ?"

She smiled. "Fair enough. The subject we have in custody out west is afraid of sharks. Great white sharks to be exact. Apparently she was traumatized by the film *Jaws*. Claims she won't even go into a swimming pool."

"Wait a minute, wait a minute," I said. "How did you find this girl? How did you get all this information?"

"One of my field operatives found her."

"So one of your employees just started going up to random women on the street and asking them if they were afraid of sharks?"

She chuckled softly. "No—it didn't have to be sharks. It could have been snakes or spiders or heights…"

"So who's the girl?" I asked. "Another hooker?"

"No. She works at a Barnes and Noble, in the section of the store where they sell music and film. That's how the subject of *Jaws* came up. The operative overheard a conversation she was having with a customer about the film."

"You can't just snatch up anyone, can you?" I said. "I mean, this girl isn't a prostitute; her disappearance won't be written off as an occupational hazard."

She pursed her lips. "Give me a little credit please. We checked her background. No living relatives. She recently moved to San Francisco from the Midwest. A loner, so to speak. It's almost too perfect."

"Do you have *any* idea how incredibly fucked up that sounded?"

She ignored me, continued with: "As I said, the girl's in custody as we speak. She's on a boat docked in the Bay area. The address is in your itinerary." She flipped her chin towards the folded papers in my hand. I looked down at them. "One of my employees has a wealth of knowledge about boats and sharks. He'll be on board with you."

I looked up from the papers. "If you've got others going then why do you need me?"

She ignored me again, kept going with her instructions. "Be sure that the girl gets a good look at the shark before you toss her overboard. It's no good if you just throw her in and she gets chomped right away. We need to milk the anticipation. That's the most crucial part of the project: filming the dread of someone coming face-to-face with their darkest fear moments before they die."

"Jesus Christ…"

"You'll be fine."

I looked at her with both venom and wonder. "I will, huh? What about you? How did you cope when you had to do it?"

She sighed again, but shocked me when she said, "We'll talk when you get back."

I stayed firm. "You won't tell me shit when I get back."

She tried to caress my face but I pulled away.

"If you cared about me at all, you'd destroy that tape and let me go," I said. "I'm your fucking prisoner and you know it. Don't pretend like it's anything else."

She looked at the floor for a beat, then raised her head and kissed me on the cheek.

Did I make a dent? Did I make a fucking dent!?

She left.

PART SEVEN

FISHING, ANYONE?

31

I needed time off work. Good news was that I had a week's vacation I hadn't used yet. Bad news was that I was an independent contractor at the spa; I didn't get paid if I didn't work. That and I was using my vacation time to feed a girl to a shark.

32

The plane ride was bearable. I slept most of the way thanks to a few plastic glasses of cheap scotch and a recent Nicholas Cage film. I had recalled seeing San Francisco portrayed in films as a city with a ton of steep hills and such, and can now say that those films were unfortunately accurate; the cheap scotch threatened reappearance all over the back of the cab driver's head if we didn't get there soon. Fortunately, we did.

"This is it?" I asked, squinting out the window towards the vast boating dock.

"This is the address you gave me," he said.

I paid, grabbed my bag, and began wandering around the dock. It was noon and hot. The sun was getting me from above and reflecting off the water from below. I was squinting and pulling at my collar the whole time I wandered.

"G'day, mate."

I turned and found myself eye to chin with one of the biggest fuckers I'd ever seen. He was deeply tanned and heavily muscled, a body attained through a lifetime of manual labor as opposed to useless beach muscles made in the gym, though I'd wager the big bugger was no stranger to hoisting iron. Oh, and in case the "G'day, mate" didn't clue you in, he was also Australian.

"You're Calvin then?" he asked.

"Yeah."

We shook hands. His grip was strong and rough.

"Call me Gene," he said. "Ever been on a boat before?"

"Couple of times."

"Right. I'll be the captain and the one locating the sharks; Andrew will be the one filming. Follow me."

He led me to the end of the dock where I was introduced to both the boat and to Andrew. The boat was like Gene—huge. Andrew was the polar opposite. The guy was a twig. He had greasy black hair and wore thick horn rims. He had a look about him that was rat-like, sleazy. If he were wearing a trench coat instead of shorts and a tee, I'd have taken his picture and posted it to Wikipedia, labeling it "sex-offender."

"So he's filming…" I said, pointing at Andrew but talking to Gene. "You're driving the boat and finding the sharks…" I splayed my hands. "And I'm…?"

Gene looked at Andrew. They exchanged funny looks. Gene looked back at me. "You're doing the deed, mate."

33

Once we'd sailed a good distance from the dock, I was introduced to the girl.

"So what ya think?" Gene asked.

The girl was bound and gagged to a chair below deck. Her hair was brown and matted, eyes brown and swollen from crying. Tee shirt and shorts, no shoes. Despite the circumstances, I could tell she was neither beautiful nor ugly. A plain Jane.

What had Angela said? From the Midwest? No family or friends? Almost too perfect? Plain only added to that "too perfect" pile. People who are plain aren't missed, even when they're alive.

(Starting to think like her now, are you?)

No. NO.

I immediately turned away from the girl. Likely sensing my apprehension, the girl began pleading through her gag—incoherent moaning and sobbing, but obvious pleading.

"I reckon she likes ya, mate!" Gene laughed with a pat on the back that pitched me forward.

I kept my back to the girl and said nothing.

"Right," Gene began, "you two keep an eye on the sheila. I'm going above to get the chum-line started."

"Got it," Andrew said, head down, fiddling with something on his camera.

Gene climbed the short wooden ladder and was gone, his heavy footsteps thumping the ceiling as he went about his business above deck.

I stole a quick glance at the girl again. Her head was down, hanging, defeated for the moment. I was grateful.

(Why? Make your job easier to have a defeated subject? No struggle? Can't blame you. Stephanie was a fucking pit bull wasn't she?)

Shut up. PLEASE Shut up.

(Make me shut up. Stop watching the fucking movie before it's too late. Do something NOW.)

I looked at Andrew. "This ever bother you?"

He kept fiddling with his camera as he responded to me. "Does what bother me?"

" *This*. What we're doing. This kind of work."

"Nah."

I snorted. "You always this cavalier about filming murder?"

He lifted his head slightly, looking up at me with mostly eyes, horn rims on the tip of his nose. We locked eyes for a tick, then he dropped his attention back to his camera and said, "It's either us or them."

What the hell is wrong with these people?

(*You mean* you *people.*)

I'm different and you know it.

(*Actions speak louder than words, superstar.*)

I headed above deck to see what Gene was doing.

34

I joined Gene above deck. He was busy ladling large spoonfuls of chum (fish guts) overboard from a large white bucket.

"It's called chum," he said with a smile after seeing my nose wrinkle from the smell.

"Yeah," I said, "I've heard of it."

He continued ladling as he spoke. "A little on the nose to us, but it's a sheila's shaved fanny to whites."

Guy would give Manny a run in the charm department.

"What about other sharks?" I asked.

"What about 'em?"

"We need a great white, right? Won't the chum attract other sharks?"

"Sure it will. But once the whites show, and we get 'em into a bit of a frenzy, the others will steer well clear."

"Frenzy?"

"That's right," Gene said. "We get 'em curious with the chum line…" He held up a big spoonful of chum, blood and guts dripping down the ladle. The smell went right up my nose and I almost barfed. "Whites can smell the tiniest bit of blood and guts from miles away." He mercifully tossed the ladle overboard and I exhaled. "Once they're curious, we toss 'em a few appetizers—keep 'em put until they get a proper meal."

I almost asked what the proper meal was—and then the sobering truth smacked me on the back of the head. So I suppose I did what I do best: I kept watching the movie—

(pathetic)

—and steered away from that sobering truth.

"What are the appetizers?" I asked.

Gene motioned towards two other white buckets a few feet away, bigger than the chum bucket. "I've got some big cunts in there. Whites aren't too choosey once you get them up to the counter. In fact, be a mate and crack one of those buckets for me. I want to get a few sorted beforehand."

I headed towards one of the big buckets, cracked the lid, and withdrew a fish that was at least three feet long and felt like it weighed as much as a kid. I handed it to Gene. "This alright?"

Gene dropped the ladle back into the chum bucket and took hold of the fish. "This'll do fine, mate." He placed the big fish onto the edge of the boat, dipped to his left, and unsheathed a giant machete fastened to his belt. With a firm grip on its handle that made his already massive forearm bulge, he braced the fish with his left and brought the blade down onto its belly with his right. The fish instantly fell in two, one piece slapping the deck, the other beneath Gene's hand on the edge of the boat.

He asked for another and I brought it to him. Same as before: fish on boat ledge; machete; *whump!* Fish in two. He asked for one more. Same process.

Finished, he sheathed the machete, organized the fish halves into a pile at his feet, and went back to the chum line.

"Who's driving the boat?" I asked.

"The ocean," he said. "We're far enough out now to let the sea take us where it wants." He flashed a sneaky smile. "Goes without saying we need a bit of privacy for this kind of thing, yeah?"

I looked at my feet.

"You alright, mate?"

I looked up. "Yeah, I'm fine. I just…I don't know what I should be doing."

Gene frowned. "I told ya; you're doing the deed, mate. You've done this before, yeah?"

"No—I mean *yeah* , but not like this. Not on a boat. Angela didn't really give me specifics about…procedure."

Gene nodded. "I gotcha. No worries then—carry on with the chum line and I'll go below deck and get the harness sorted on the sheila."

"The harness?"

"That's right. We've got us a fishing pole." He pointed to a large metal pole attached to the roof of the cabin. The pole did not stand up straight like a flag pole; it was fixed horizontally, pointing out towards the sea. Its height was maybe a good ten feet from the deck, like a pull-up bar for giants. (Gene probably used it.)

I'd barely noticed the pole when boarding because I had no clue what should, and should not be on a boat like this. As I studied the pole now, I saw that it was segmented, capable of extension. I also saw a pulley system that ran the length of the pole, the tip ending in a big wheel that fed the line, the base ending with two large cranks. Had Gene not told me what it was, I would have assumed it was a pulley system rigged for a sail or something. Like I said; I didn't know boats.

"I don't get it," I said. "I thought we were just pushing her overboard."

"Nah—what fun would that be? We'll get her all rigged and she'll be a nice juicy worm on a hook for Jawsy." He smiled and winked at me.

I looked away and could not help muttering, "*Jesus…*"

Gene inched towards me. I looked at him and saw concern on his face. It wasn't friendly concern. "You won't be losing your nerve come kick off time, will you, mate?"

I looked away again, shook my head.

"I hope not," he said. He nudged me, insisting I meet his unyielding gaze. "For your sake."

35

I had just cracked open the third chum barrel and ladled out two spoons when Gene came up from below and approached.

"I reckon that'll do for now, mate," he said, taking the ladle from me and dropping it into one of the empty buckets.

"What's up with the girl?" I asked.

He flicked his chin towards the cabin. "Go on down and have a look if you like."

I did.

The girl was still tied to the chair; still bound and gagged, but was now wearing the harness. It looked like a parachute to me.

Andrew came up on my left. "All gift-wrapped and ready to go," he said. "All we have to do now is wait for *dun-dun-dun-dun…dun-dun-dun-dun…*"

John Williams' classic theme to *Jaws*. The sick fucker—Andrew, not John Williams—wore a maniacal grin as he performed, his face inches from the girl's, his "*dun-dun-dun-duns*" getting louder and louder, his black eyes behind those horn rims wilder and wilder.

The girl was damn near having a seizure; sobbing and screeching into the gag as Andrew carried on.

Andrew suddenly stopped, stood upright. "Fuck! This is *gold*, man. I need to be getting this shit." He grabbed his camera, fiddled with a few things, then shoved the lens into the girl's face. "Come on, honey, make love to the camera for me…" The girl kept turning her head away from the lens, but Andrew was undeterred; he followed her every move, started giggling as he continued to taunt. "Give me scared…oh, oh yeah, yeah that's good." Giggle. "*Visualize* for me, baby. Picture the *biggest* fucking shark you can…" Giggle. "Now picture that scary son of a bitch chompin' down on you like a fucking meatloaf!"

I placed my hand over the lens and guided it towards the floor.

"Hey!" he screamed. "What the fuck?"

Calmly, I said, "I don't want you getting my face on film."

"So then put your fucking mask on!"

I got in his face. "Easy, man; I don't like the way you're talking to me."

I saw him swallow hard, his Adam's apple bobbing in his scrawny neck.

"You're supposed to be doing a job," he said, his tone softer.

"I understand that," I said, my voice still calm but firm. "But when you start getting excited, waving that camera all around, you might end up with a shot of my profile, and I really don't want that."

He swallowed again. "But the job's all about fear; we gotta get her scared."

I glanced back at the girl. The fact that her heart hadn't burst from her chest was nothing short of a miracle. "I think she's plenty fucking scared, asshole."

Andrew turned his back to me and set his camera on the shelf. Perhaps in an attempt at salvaging some sense of pride, he turned back and asked, "You *do* have a mask, right?"

I did. Angela had given me a hood this time. Like an executioner's hood. Like the one I remembered seeing in her lovely montage. I'd taken it from my bag and shoved it into my back pocket soon after I was below deck.

"Yeah—I got one," I said.

"Maybe you should get it ready then."

"Maybe you should shut up before I start beating you with your own camera."

"You wouldn't say that shit if Gene was here."

"You gonna go run and cry to him?"

"I'm just sayin', you wouldn't—"

Gene boomed from above, cutting Andrew off. His shouts were loud and clear and they chilled me. The movie I was watching had hit a pivotal scene.

Gene yelled: " *WE'VE GOT ONE!* "

36

Andrew and I hurried up the cabin steps and joined Gene by the edge of the boat. His eyes were wide and intense as he looked down at the water. I followed his gaze and looked down.

"I don't see anything," I said.

Gene smirked at me, took one of the fish halves, and tossed it overboard.

There was a brief moment where the dead fish floated on the surface as though it would eventually drift away untouched. The water appeared so dark and still, I felt that anything below had surely gone. I was seconds from voicing this when a monster's mouth emerged from the deep blue without warning, impossibly wide, unsheathing rows of white knives, slamming shut on the fish, taking it whole.

I jumped back, nearly tumbling over my own feet. " *Jesus Christ!* "

Gene exploded with laughter and slapped another heavy hand on my back. "He's a big one, ain't he, mate? I'd say a good fifteen footer."

My heart hammered in my chest. I'd never had a problem with sharks and *I* was about to shit myself. This girl was going to have a fucking coronary before we even got her into the water.

(*So you're definitely going through with it then?*)

Gene tossed two more fish halves overboard. Andrew's camera was on the shark's whereabouts, had been the whole time. I wondered if the sick bastard flinched like I did when the bear trap with fins appeared.

"Right," Gene began, "Andrew, turn the camera off for now while we get her on the hook." He looked at me. "Go on below and grab your mask and the sheila. You need any help with her, give me a shout. I'm going to stay here and make sure Jawsy stays interested."

(*Do something.*)

Like what?

(*Hit the bastard! Toss him overboard.*)

He's a fucking house.

(*Just hit him! And KEEP hitting until he's in a fucking coma, then hit him some more.)*

"Calvin!"

I flinched and my daze broke. Gene was frowning, spearing me with his eyes. For some reason, I muttered, "What?"

"The fuck ya mean, ' *what* '?"

(*Hit him hit him hit him hit him*)

I looked at his jaw. The thing was huge, no way I'd miss.

(*Hit him hit him hit him hit him*)

Gene shoved me back a step. "Well go on!"

I turned and headed below deck.

(*You useless…*)

37

The girl started a desperate struggle with her binds the moment I arrived. The harness Gene had wrapped her in was still fastened tight; all I needed to do was untie her and bring her up so she could be attached to a giant fishing pole.

The gag in the girl's mouth prevented her from any sensible dialogue, but it did not stop her from trying. She eventually resorted to sobbing the word please over and over (it came out sounding like "leez") as though each utterance might carry more impact than the last. And it did.

"Shut up," I said. "If you just shut up it'll be easier."

" *Leez.* "

Don't look in her eyes. Start untying her binds.

(Pathetic…)

"*Leeeez…*"

Almost done. You don't hear a thing.

(Pathetic piece of…)

" *LEEEEEEEZ…* "

" *Shut up!* " I grabbed her throat with my left and cocked my right.

She did shut up, but not out of fear. Not because she thought I'd hit her. She shut up because she could see it. Could see that I was doing it all against my will. Probably saw it from the start. She stared into me now with eyes that no longer begged for mercy, but asked for it. There was a difference. And even after her realization, those eyes did not convey relief or victory, they were wise; they embraced the truth of our situation, spoke with soulful blinks and focused appeals to my humanity: I could not even bring myself to hit this woman, yet I was to feed her to a shark?

I slowly took my hand off her throat and lowered my fist. We stared at each other; that new gaze of hers louder than her pleading had ever been.

Gene from above: " *Calvin! Let's go, mate!* "

(What are you going to do?)

Aloud, I said: "I don't know."

The girl frowned, looked at me quizzically.

(Go up there and end this.)

"How?"

The girl frowned some more, even looked over both shoulders to be sure someone else wasn't below deck.

" *How?* " I said again.

The girl tried talking through her gag, an upward inflection in her tone, likely asking me what the hell I was talking about.

(You can do this, man.)

"Yeah."

(You can still make it right.)

"Yeah."

Gene's heavy feet suddenly thundering down the cabin stairs. " *For fuck's sake!* "

He shoved me to one side, untied the girl, and heaved her over his shoulder. She began screaming and kicking at once. He thundered back upstairs. I followed.

"I don't know what you're playing at mate," he began, furiously attaching the girl's harness to the series of thick ropes hanging from the wheeled-end of the pole, her struggles and swipes against his work futile, a child fighting an adult. "But you better pay attention right fucking now…"

Gene stomped towards the cabin, towards the cranks that operated the pole. He flipped a large metallic latch and began operating one of the cranks. The girl's feet left the deck as she began to rise. Desperate kicks and screams during the ascent.

"You watching?" he asked me.

The girl was now several feet above deck, legs constantly flailing, muffled screams relentless. Gene flipped another latch and began working the second crank, this one extending the segmented pole, guiding the girl out to sea.

Before long she was truly a worm on a hook, dangling overboard, her toes ten feet from the water. She looked down and screeched—a shrill, piercing sound, like blasts from a whistle. Streams of urine started down her bare legs and dripped into the sea.

I don't know what she saw, I couldn't see from where I stood. Maybe it was the shark. Maybe ten sharks. Or maybe none. Maybe none was worse. Looking down into the chum-red water, knowing your darkest nightmare lurked somewhere below, waiting for you.

(Unless you stop it.)

Gene turned back to me. "Were you watching? Were you fucking watching me do it?"

I nodded.

(You were watching—watching the fucking movie. Make it right, Calvin.)

Gene spun. "Andrew! Camera ready?"

Andrew gave a thumbs up.

Gene spun back to me. "Right, when he starts filming, you lower her into the water like I showed you. Let her toes skim the surface, but no deeper. Try and tease the bastard if you can. If it looks like he's about to take a nibble, jerk her up; let her keep seeing what's waiting below. We want to milk this fear shit as much as we can. If the big cunt *does* manage a bite then bring what's left of her back up—we want to get all the gory bits on camera. I'll let you know when we drop her for good. Where's your mask?"

I took the hood from my back pocket and showed it to him.

"I'll tell you something else, mate," he said, "no fucking way are we getting equal splits when this is done. You've done fuck all this whole time."

He backed away, left me to the cranks. Turned to Andrew and screamed: "Stand by!"

I didn't move.

Gene screamed at me: " Put ya fucking mask on! "

I looked up at the girl. Her face was a sickly white, fear syphoning all blood. Her body convulsed as if in the throes of a seizure. More urine flowed down her legs. Over and over again she cried: *"Leez, God! Leez, God! Leez, God!"*

I dropped the hood.

Gene stormed over, shoved me back. "You weak fucking cunt."

He picked up the hood and put it on. Began operating the cranks.

"LEEZ, GOD!!! LEEZ, GOD!!!"

(*Do something.*)

The girl started to descend.

(*DO something.*)

"OH GOD, LEEEEEEEEEEEEZZZZ!!!"

(*DO SOMETHING, YOU GUTLESS FUCKING—*)

I hit Gene with the hardest punch I'd ever thrown. The hood made it hard to get my accuracy right; I prayed I got his jaw.

He flew backwards, landing heavily onto the deck.

The girl's descent came to a jarring halt. She dangled a good five feet from the water. Still safe.

Gene sat up, removed the hood and smiled. "I see," he said, rubbing his chin. Apparently I *had* hit him on the jaw, but the tough bastard took it like a slap. "This is how you want it then, yeah?"

He got to his feet and removed his shirt, fanning out his massive torso. He grinned and started forward, fists clenching and unclenching, dying to get a hold of me.

I backed up, frantically looking around for anything I could get my hands on.

"No one's helping ya, mate," he said, grin widening. "You've made your fucking bed…"

Unbelievably, Gene's size became an asset for me. He was slow. I could see him angling his body sideways to load up with a big right hand. I beat him to the punch and fired a quick jab with my fingertips into his eyes. I didn't actually get my fingers *into* his eyes, but I did swipe the general area, causing him to flinch and giving me the precious second I needed to punt his nuts up into his throat. He doubled over and groaned, but as I moved in for a second punt to his head, the big fucker lunged forward and caught my leg, lifting me up over his shoulder.

I struggled like a cat on a leash as I believed I would be heaved overboard, but to my relief (sort of) I was slammed back down onto the deck with Gene's full weight on top of me. My breath vanished and for a second I saw black.

I fought to regain consciousness and instantly covered my head. Gene drew his fist back like a club and hammered it into my guard. The impact was so great it drove my forearms into my face, jarring me as much as any decent shot I'd taken over the years. One or two more of those and he'd break through my defense and put me out.

I started bucking my hips wildly, but he was just too big; he wasn't going anywhere and neither was I. He reared back, the second sledgehammer ready to come down.

And then he stopped.

Giant fist suspended in the air, head now turned to the left, Gene was staring at Andrew…who was filming us.

Gene screamed: " *What the fuck ya doing!?* "

Still filming, Andrew said, "This is awesome!"

" *Don't film my face, ya fucking dickhead!* "

Gene's outrage at Andrew's idiocy had momentarily taken his attention off of me, and I used that moment to frantically search for a means of escape. I had felt this means all along but had failed to register its presence as the worry of Gene's fists superseded all. Now, that means was presenting itself with wonderful clarity as it continued its constant jabbing into my leg. It was Gene's machete. Why he never pulled the thing out and used it himself I'll never know and I didn't care, but it was there, dangling on his hip, poking me in the leg, and the blessed thing was even unfastened.

In one swift motion, I jerked the machete free. Gene immediately took his eyes off of Andrew and looked down at me. Before he could react I gripped the machete handle with both hands and plunged the big blade deep into his belly.

Gene grimaced and groaned as if taking a painful shit. He rolled off of me and lay on his back, grimacing and groaning some more, periodically clutching at the machete standing tall from his abdomen.

I wasted no time. I scrambled to my feet, yanked the machete from his gut, and brought the thing whistling down into his skull.

I stood panting, staring down at Gene, the machete stuck in his skull, eyes open and lifeless, blood beginning to pool beneath his head. One of his massive legs twitched involuntarily.

I then felt something thud into the back of my head. It wasn't too hard, more annoying. I turned to find Andrew squared up to me in a lame fighting stance, his pigeon chest heaving with fear. The scrawny prick had taken a cheap shot at me.

I can't be certain, but I'm pretty sure I was smiling when I cracked him. One shot, a right cross on the point of the chin, launched him off his feet and onto the deck in an unconscious heap. His body went rigid as it seized, and he made that gurgling sound the recently-knocked-the-fuck-out often make, the one that sounds like a snore.

I rushed towards the edge of the boat. The girl was still on the hook, still dangling a good five feet from the water.

"I'm going to help you!" I shouted. It felt good to say. I said it again. "I'm going to help you! Just hold on, okay?"

She nodded eagerly.

I hurried to the cranks. I flipped the lever, gripped the handle with both hands and glanced over my shoulder at her. "You ready?"

She nodded eagerly again.

I turned back and completed one full crank.

An explosion of water, the screeching sound of wrenching metal, and the handle jerked violently from my hands, knocking me back a step. I immediately spun towards the girl. Only the top half remained.

"*No,*" I whispered to no one.

I ran to the edge of the boat. Chunks of flesh and blood fell from the girl's severed torso, splashing lightly into the sea. I peered over the boat's edge. The ocean was already turning a dark red. A huge dorsal fin sliced the red water.

"No!" I screamed at the water, as though it had betrayed me.

I looked at the girl again. Her head now lolled to one side, eyes still open but seeing nothing. The color of her skin was already beginning to gray from the rapid blood loss.

I knew I had to dump her remains overboard, but I took my time about it. Crazy as it may sound, the longer she hung from that harness, the less I felt I had completely

(*what?*)

failed.

(*You did fail.*)

No, I—

(*You waited too long.*)

I brought both hands to my head as though trying to crush it, screamed

" *FUCK* " until my throat seized.

Quickly, blocking every thought banging on the door to get in, I turned my back on the girl, went to Gene, pulled the machete from his head, went to the cranks, and chopped the connecting ropes that supported the girl. The splash of her torso into the sea behind me was like a gut kick. I heard more splashing shortly after, and I suspected (knew) what it was, and a second gut kick was my prize.

I glanced at Gene.

What had he said about working them into a frenzy? Keeping them interested until they get a proper meal?

I rolled Gene's big body overboard. "A proper meal," I said to his floating corpse. "How's that for a slice of irony, ya big fuck?"

I heard a sudden moaning behind me. I spun and saw Andrew coming to. I couldn't remember if I'd smiled when I'd knocked him out, but I am absolutely positive I was smiling—no, *grinning* —when I grabbed the scrawny prick by his hair, dragged him towards the edge of the boat, and pitched him overboard. Couple that with the fact that he'd regained his senses by the time he hit the water, and I was all but giggling as I watched him scream and flail in that sea of red.

" *Dun-dun-dun-dun…!* " I called to him. I then bent, snatched his camera, smashed it repeatedly on the deck, and tossed it overboard. "Here's your camera, man."

Andrew's fear was electric. He bobbed and choked, head whipping in all directions, desperate to locate the monster beneath.

"Oh he's down there, man," I said. "He's down there."

"I'll give you whatever you want!" he cried. " *Anything!* "

I resumed singing as I turned my back on him. " *Dun-dun-dun-dun…* "

* * *

I'd seen a few of those disaster films where regular folks had to land planes when the pilot got sick or died or whatever, and I can distinctly remember thinking, *God, that would suck* . Well, although a boat may not be as dire a situation as a plane, I can tell you that steering, and especially docking one still sucks pretty hard when your knowledge of boats goes back to when you played with one in the tub.

Fortunately, I did eventually find a dock in some obscure spot behind someone's palatial home. I didn't even bother trying to tie the fucker up, just hopped off while it was still moving. This, of course, resulted in the boat colliding with the dock and its supporting structures, which, in turn, resulted in a very pissed off homeowner storming out of said palatial home and towards yours truly.

The man approached, screaming and hollering. " *What the hell do you think you're doing, you dumb son of a——"*

Without missing a stride, I knocked the guy clean out with a left hook and kept on walking. Dick move, I know, but I was in no mood.

38

I was in a cab, headed back to San Francisco International Airport when I decided I couldn't wait. I had to call Angela.

"How'd it go?" she answered.

"Not too good."

"Why, what happened?"

"I couldn't do it."

"So who did?"

"Nobody."

"Nobody?"

"That's right—it didn't get done."

"I see. And Gene and Andrew were okay with that?"

"Gene seemed a little upset. It's irrelevant now though."

"Irrelevant, huh?" A pause. "They're dead, aren't they?"

"Yup."

"You killed them?"

"Yup."

"What about the girl?"

I clenched my teeth and took a deep breath through my nose to steady myself. God, how I wished she was still alive. Alive and sitting next to me. I'd put her on the goddamn phone. Have her say hello to the old ringmaster herself.

"She's dead," I eventually said.

"So something *did* happen?"

"No—not like you think. It was an accident."

"Some people say there are no accidents, Calvin."

"Yeah, well those people have obviously never seen a great white shark leap out of the water and bite a girl in half before."

The cab driver shot a nervous glance over his shoulder.

"Wow," Angela said. "Did you get it on film?"

"Nope—tossed it overboard," I said with what little joy I could summon.

Another pause. And then: "So let me get this straight. Gene and Andrew are dead."

"Yup.

"The girl is dead."

"Yes."

"And we've got no tape."

"Correct.

"So we've got nothing."

"No, *you've* got nothing. I'm done. I am *fucking done* ."

"You're done, huh?" she said. "Just like that?"

"Just like that."

"So I guess you're not afraid of prison anymore."

"Fuck you, bitch. Send your little tape to whoever you want. I'll take my chances."

She chuckled. "Sorry, Calvin, it's not that easy. You can't just—"

" *Easy?* I killed *four-fucking-people* this week! I—" I stopped suddenly, a realization hitting me like a horrible memory once forgotten. "Holy shit...you only need to kill *three* people in order to be officially labeled a serial killer... *I'm a fucking serial killer!* "

The cab driver glanced back at me again. He looked like he was about to shit himself.

"Relax, Calvin, okay? You need to calm—"

" *Stop telling me to relax and calm down!* I'm done, you hear me!? I am fucking done!"

"Okay, okay, I'm sorry..." She stammered, incredulously stumped for words. "You can't just...you can't..." She shifted suddenly, making a weak attempt at regaining the advantage by targeting my psyche. "You know what? I don't think you *are* done." Even over the phone I could tell her words weren't loaded. "I *saw* something in you. I saw—"

I barked out a laugh, cutting her off.

"What you saw was *depression* , Angela—plain and simple. I think, and I say things that are conceivable only in the safety of my own fucked-up head, and that's all." I shifted the phone to my other ear as I started building momentum. "I used to think there'd be no significant transition if my depraved thoughts ever crossed over into reality, but you know what? There's a big one. *A big-fucking-terrifying transition.* And now, thanks to a sick bitch like you, I know that as an absolute *fact* ."

A long pause. When she finally spoke she sounded so vulnerable, I wondered if it was even her. "Please don't do this. I'll tell you everything, okay? Just please don't leave... *Please* ."

"You had your chance to talk to me. I'm done." I snapped my phone shut.

(Impressive.)

Shut the fuck up.

I leaned forward in my seat. "How much further?"

"Not far, not far," the cabbie said quickly, probably counting the seconds before we hit the airport.

"Good. Hurry up. And don't mess with me; I'm a serial killer."

PART EIGHT

THE TOOTH SHALL SET YOU FREE

39

It felt good to stand up to Angela. All that pride and defiance, telling her to fuck off, despite her pleading.

Her pleading. What was all that about? I'm no shrink, and if you haven't guessed by now, I'm the reigning champ of cynicism, but it felt like there was something sincere in her tone that, for a record first, was not the starts of a mind fuck. She truly seemed upset about something, and I know it wasn't the prospect of losing me as a lover; in addition to holding the Cynicism Belt, I am also number one contender for the Lack of Self-esteem Title.

So what was it then? What did she seem so upset about? And more importantly— *far* more importantly—what to do about the tape? Angela seemed upset on the phone, but how soon until that sadness turns to anger? How soon until she follows through on her blackmail threat and FedExes copies of that tape to every precinct in the Philadelphia area?

I stuck my key in my apartment door.

Do I run? Could I run?

(*Or maybe you could eliminate the problem at the source.*)

She wouldn't give me the tape.

(*You know that's not what I meant. Your body count is all her fault anyway. What's one more?*)

No. No more…

(*It would be even* more *justified than when you killed the freak in self-defense. It's all about self-preservation.*)

NO. Besides, she made it abundantly clear that she's not the only one with a copy of the tape. If anything happened to her…

(*She said you have no way of KNOWING if someone else has the tape. That you'd be taking a big risk. She could have been bluffing.*)

Drop it.

I entered my apartment and Pele rushed towards my shins, meowing incessantly as he rubbed against them—a hello and a where the fuck have you been?

I bent to pick him up, but he moved out of range. He circled then cast me a look with another meow that was English to me: *Fuck you; you think I'm forgiving you so quickly? Get on my dinner, bitch, and MAYBE I'll let you pet me later.*

I headed to my kitchen with two objectives: feed Pele, and whiskey Calvin.

Pele was soon nose deep in a bowl of Friskies, and I was soon nose deep in a healthy glass of Beam. I leaned against my kitchen counter as I drank.

Run or wait? That's what it all comes down to, doesn't it?

(Or...)

I said drop it—it's not an option.

I downed the remainder of my Beam, poured myself another, and then headed towards my sofa. Although I knew I wouldn't pay attention to program one, the simple act of channel surfing might be cathartic in a let's-figure-out-how-to-get-out-of-the-snuff film industry-without-going-to-prison kind of way.

I set my drink on the arm of the sofa and leaned forward to grab the remote from the coffee table.

I froze, my hand suspended in air, hovering over the remote.

What...the fuck...are those?

I needed a better look—because they couldn't have been what I thought they were. Slowly, steadily, I lifted the remote by its sides, keeping it horizontal so as not to spill anything.

I brought the remote closer. Yup—two blood-stained teeth resting on the remote like capers on a biscuit.

I dropped the remote as if it had just burned me, the teeth scattering across my rug. Pele approached one of the teeth, sniffed, and then started batting it playfully.

"No! Pele, *no* !" I leapt from the sofa and shooed him away from the tooth. He hissed and swiped at my foot before darting off.

Everything felt like a scene in a movie, where the camera does a dizzying 360 around the main character as he desperately clings to sanity.

A sudden knock at my door stops the camera's orbit cold, and now it's a shotgun zoom in on my panicked face with the classic tilted frame to convey my instability.

I faced my door, chest heaving, mind spiraling. "Who is it?"

"I need help." A female voice. Soft and weak.

" *Who is it?* "

"Please let me in."

I inched cautiously towards the door as if it might burst open at any second. I placed an eye on the peephole. It was Angela. Her head was down, and she had something pressed to her mouth, but it was her.

"Angela?"

"Please let me in, Calvin."

A trick. Was it a trick? Were there freaks with her, flanking her, far enough away so I missed them through the peephole? Would there be no blackmail after all? In its stead, a sweeping under the rug, like I had been tricked to do with the freak for having a big mouth?

"Are you alone?" I asked.

"Yes."

I looked through the peephole again. Strained muscles in my eye I'd never used in order to gain the widest scope possible. She did seem alone. And if she did have goons with her, wouldn't they just kick the door down? Kill me and be gone before neighbors started to wonder what all the commotion was about?

I opened the door. The thing covering her mouth was a white rag. At least it used to be white. Now it was mostly red. I pulled her inside, shut the door and locked it.

I gestured towards the rag. "Are you hurt? What happened?"

She pulled the bloodied cloth away from her mouth, winced and raised her upper lip. I now knew whose front teeth were on my remote.

"Jesus Christ. Who did that to you?"

"My—" She stopped, sighed, and then corrected herself. " *Our* boss."

40

Angela sat on my sofa. The bleeding had more or less stopped, so I tossed the bloodied rag and gave her a damp washcloth from my bathroom. She nodded her appreciation and periodically dabbed the cloth on the raw gap, wincing each time. I sat on the coffee table, across from her.

"So you're saying you answer to someone," I said. "This isn't just your gig."

Cloth to mouth, she nodded slowly.

"So this is what you meant when you said you had no choice in doing this kind of work. I *wasn't* misunderstanding things."

She nodded again and lowered the rag. "I may be a bit wild, Calvin, but I'm not a psychopath. I was fucked...just like I fucked you."

"Blackmailed."

"More or less."

I stared at her, refusing to blink, lips pursed in contempt. *Start talking* , I hoped my face read.

She took a deep breath and let it out with a long sigh. "Okay...you ready for the after school special?"

I nodded.

She dabbed her mouth with the cloth and let out another long sigh. "I was an addict and I lived on the street. My life sucked and I wanted to die. So I OD'd. But then some Good Samaritan comes along, scoops me up, and dumps me off at the hospital. Saves my life.

"A few days later I'm released, and as I'm leaving I'm greeted by a limo. The guy inside tells me *he* was the one who saved me. Tells me I was so beautiful with all this potential and that if I let him, he would take care of me." She dabbed her mouth again and winced. "My life is a big fucking zero so I figure I've got nothing to lose, right? So I go with him, and for a year he's like Mr. Johnny-on-the-spot with the luxury and spoils. I'm living in a palace, new clothes, jewelry...I don't even have any desire for smack anymore.

"And I never questioned it either. I mean why look a gift horse in the mouth, right? It's been over a year already, and I figured if the guy just wanted to fuck me he would have tried by now. Instead he just treats me like a princess and gives me whatever I want."

"But...?"

She held up a hand, asking for my patience. "So there I am, living a dream life. But after a while I start to ask myself all those questions I wasn't asking in the beginning. Why is this guy doing all this for me? Can there really be no ulterior motive? So one day I ask him. And he told me."

"Told you what?"

"Told me the kind of work that he did—and that he was planning on using me in that line of work."

"Use you how?"

"Recruiting. Bringing in people for us to employ, and bringing in people for us to...film."

"So what did you do after he told you everything?"

"I freaked. I called him a sick bastard and said I was leaving."

"You did?"

She frowned a little. " *Yes*. I told you, I'm not a psychopath."

I held up a hand, a slightly patronizing hint to my tone when I said: "My apologies."

Her little frown grew. "Should I even go on?"

I wanted her to. Whether I was swallowing all of it—

So then who pulled out her teeth?

—or not, I wasn't sure, but I did want her to go on.

"Yeah," I said. "Yeah, go on."

She paused, taking her time dabbing her mouth, likely reminding me that both of her front teeth had been ripped out, thank you very much; a little courtesy would be nice.

I reiterated with a teaspoon of that courtesy. "No really, please—go on. I'm sorry. Tell me what he did when you told him you were leaving."

She did a final dab and said, "He beat the shit out of me."

My face must have registered surprise, because she continued with: "Yeah—he told me that he didn't spend the past year wasting his money on a junkie like me so that she could just up and leave whenever she wanted to."

"You ever try sneaking away, or...?"

"Several times. He always found me though. And every time I was brought back I was showed the error of my ways. Once he locked me in a cellar for a week with no food, only water. Told me I could stand to lose a few pounds anyway." She gave a pathetic chuckle.

"So I guess you stopped trying to run after that?"

"No—I tried one last time. Of course I was caught and brought back, but this time he didn't punish me; he just showed me a picture."

"Of what?"

"A beautiful woman lying by a pool. He told me it was the girl I was replacing. He then shows me another photo, and I can tell it's the same girl, but just barely. She was hanging on a meat hook."

"Jesus."

"He told me that she too had tried to leave several times, and that if I tried once more I'd be hanging on a hook next to her."

"So what'd you do?"

She shrugged. "What could I do? I stayed."

"How long ago was this?"

"Five years, give or take."

"*Five years?*"

She gave a reluctant nod.

"Does he still abuse you?"

"Not if I do what I'm told. Every now and then I'll get a little courage and defy him, but I always end up regretting it." Another pathetic chuckle. "I think it's a safe bet to say that my only way out is that meat hook."

It added up and it didn't.

"Wait, wait, wait," I said. "You weren't necessarily acting like a woman who was doing this shit against her will. Hell, you had me believing you were Charles Manson's hot sister."

She pursed her lips at my wit. "I became *desensitized* , Calvin. And let's be honest, the money helped."

"Doesn't mean you have to like it."

"I *don't* like it. I got used to it. I got used to playing the part."

I splayed my hands. "Okay—so then if what you're saying is true, then what you were doing with me was just a job, recruiting. Old Manny was right after all. What number does that make me?"

"Stop it. It's not just a job with you. I had—I *have* feelings for you."

"Please."

"It's true. Yes, I fucked with you, and yes, I brought you into this…world, but I did it because I liked you, and I did it because…"

"Because what?"

"…Because I thought you could help me."

"Oh what, you want me to feed a co-ed to an alligator or something?"

"Make all the jokes you want. The simple truth is that I wanted out from the beginning, but I couldn't get out. So I did what I was told. Then I met you. And I liked you. And you seemed perfect. You were perfect to bring on board, and you were perfect for me. Yes, I was being selfish, but I truly sensed something in you. I—"

I held up a hand, cutting her off. "Okay, you need to *stop* with all this 'sensing' and 'seeing' shit in me. All you did was exploit my demons. Don't make it out to be anything else."

"No, it wasn't—" She stopped and sighed. "Okay, yes, I did; I admit it. I'm terrible for what I put you through, I won't ever deny that. But I did *not* fake any of our passion, okay? It was real. I just didn't want to be alone in this nightmare anymore. I wanted someone I could trust, and someone I liked, and...someone who could maybe do me the greatest favor of all."

"I told you I was done, Angela. I meant it."

She leaned forward and flashed the gap where her front teeth used to be. "Look at me. This is because I told him the job at sea was botched and that you were quitting. He wanted you dead— *immediately* . I begged him not to. So he took my teeth as punishment, and then told me I had one week to convince you to stay on board."

"Or what?"

"My guess? We *both* end up on a meat hook."

"Your teeth..." I said. "They're here. They were sitting on my remote. Who put them there?"

She gave me a look. "Who do you think?"

"He was here? In my apartment?"

"He wants you to know that he can get to you whenever he wants."

I looked around my apartment. The thought of a guy like that—or likely, his thugs—being in my place made it feel haunted.

And then a thought hit me. A word actually. *Favor.* She kept mentioning a favor she wanted from me. I knew what it was almost instantly.

"You want me to kill him, don't you?" I said.

She did not hesitate with her response. "You'd be helping both of us."

"It can't be that simple. I imagine a guy like that isn't easy to get to. Besides, you can't convince me someone hasn't tried offing a piece of shit like him before."

"Not someone like you."

"I'd rather you stroke my dick than my ego, thank you very much."

"I'm not kidding, Calvin. Yes, he's tough to get to, but that's mostly because few people know who he is. The few who *do* know are either terrified of him or worship him." She paused to allow impact for the words to come. " *I* know who he is. And *I* know more about him than almost anyone."

"I see," I said. "You got the brains and I got the brawn, that it?"

"No—we've *both* got the brains; *you've* got the brawn. I've seen you in action, and lord knows I've picked your brain enough. You're physically capable to handle most extremities, and you're no idiot."

"You talk about this like it's a movie," I said. "I'm not Arnold or Stallone. I'm a fucking massage therapist who can throw a decent punch."

"You underestimate yourself."

"You overestimate myself."

"I wouldn't be suggesting this if I didn't think it was possible."

"You're suggesting this to save your ass."

"I'm suggesting this to save *our* asses. That is unless you want to keep doing this stuff the rest of your life."

"You really think killing this guy is the only option?"

She splayed a hand. "I'm open to suggestions if you got 'em."

"Run," I said.

"I told you, I tried that."

" *I* could run," I said.

She did not appear angry or hurt. She appeared as if she was expecting my show of defiance, half-hearted as it admittedly was.

"Yeah, you could do that. And let's assume he followed through with his threat and got rid of me. You think he wouldn't go looking for you soon after? You think he'd let you just wander off and hope you kept quiet about his little enterprise?"

I said nothing.

"You want to spend the rest of your life looking over your shoulder?"

Obviously I didn't, but the idea of someone like me killing some shadowy kingpin like Mr. Johnny-on-the-spot seemed way too fiction to me.

"Okay," I said. "Let's say we can pull it off. What then?"

"What do you mean?"

"I mean *what then* ?"

She frowned and squinted, confused. "There is no *then* . It would be over; we'd be free."

"Free to go our separate ways?"

"Oh...that 'what then?'" She studied me. "Are you asking if there's going to be an 'us' after it's over?"

"No, not really..."

(*Yes really*)

"...I just wanted to know what you had planned, that's all."

She nodded slowly, face even, obviously seeing my feeble digging for what it was, yet sparing me the

(*well deserved*)

acknowledgment of the peril she'd just placed my king.

(*You have no king. Your whole board is full of pawns.*)

"I was thinking retirement," she said. "You *and* me."

HA!

(*HA what? You forgetting who this is?*)

"Massage therapists don't have much of a pension," I said.

"You wouldn't need one," she said. "He's loaded, Calvin. It'd be like two birds with one stone."

(*Aaannnd there it is.*)

Fuck.

"You must think I'm a fucking idiot," I said.

"What?"

"This is *Thriller Fiction 101* , Angela. I take out Mr. John; steal his money; and then get bent over by some sexy bitch who's been playing me like a fiddle the whole fucking time."

"Playing you? I'm sorry; did I pull my *own* teeth out?" She flashed her toothless grimace to hammer it home. "Besides, the money I made this past *year* is more than you'll ever see in a lifetime."

"Thanks."

"I don't need money, Calvin—I need freedom. So do you. But if the money's going to be there, I say why not take it?"

"How would I get into his home? I would imagine a guy like that has crazy security."

"He does, but you wouldn't be going to his home. You'd be going to a club—one of those men's spas where the stinking rich go after work to soak in hot tubs and sip brandy. Mr. John always goes after hours when the place is empty. Special privileges for the stinking rich."

"You have a key to the place?"

She nodded.

"Of course you do. What about the money? You gonna tell me he keeps all his money at this club?"

"Of course not. But some of it'll be there. He uses the club to make deposits for him. It helps filter his income while maintaining anonymity. He brings the money with him and leaves it there over night."

"How much will be there?"

"Enough for you and me to have the fairy-tale ending."

(*Fairy tales are violent as all hell. There's probably more truth in what she's saying than she even realizes.*)

"So you're telling me all I have to do is go into this place after hours, find Mr. John soaking in a tub, kill him, steal his money, and then just stroll on out? It can't be that easy."

"It won't be. Vlad and Yuri will be with him."

"Who the hell are Vlad and Yuri?"

"His protection. His shadows, basically. Brothers who came over from Russia to help with certain job-related…things."

"These guys are badasses?"

She went to answer, stopped, sighed, and then gave a reluctant: "Yes."

I felt a tingle of adrenaline. "What can you tell me about them?"

"I don't know too much. They look alike. Bald, built like trucks, no necks. The tattoos always helped telling them apart."

"What do you mean?"

"It's weird—one's *covered* in tattoos, and the other doesn't have a single mark." She dabbed her mouth and added: "Their ears are gross."

"Huh?"

"They have gross ears. They're all thick and lumpy like—"

"Cauliflower," I blurted. "They have cauliflower ears."

She thought for a second, then looked at me as though impressed with my input. "Yeah, they *do* kinda look like cauliflower."

"No, I'm not trying to help you find the right descriptor for their fucking ears, I'm saying—" I groaned; I didn't feel like giving an explanation for the cause and effects of cauliflower ear, so I skipped right to the end. "I'm saying they're obviously grapplers, yes?"

"Grapplers?"

I was getting irritated. "Wrestlers? People who tie you up in fucking knots...?"

"Oh," she said softly. "Yeah, they were wrestlers—I think Mr. John said they competed in the Olympic trials a few years back. I think they were also champions in something else."

"Sambo?"

"Yeah, that's it." She frowned, curious. "How did you know that?"

I spoke without taking a breath: "Because it's a badass Russian grappling art. Fedor Emelianenko? Greatest heavyweight that ever lived? His primary style was Sambo."

"I...don't understand a word you just said."

I closed my eyes, exhaled, and started rubbing my temples. "Forget it." I opened my eyes, exhaled again. "So how'd these guys find their way here? With Mr. John?"

She shrugged. "I'm not really sure. From what I understand, they kind of *had* to leave, if you know what I mean."

"Yes," I said with no satisfaction, "unfortunately I do. What happened?"

She shrugged again. "Like I said; I'm not really sure. I *do* know they got into trouble not long after arriving here. That's how Mr. John found them."

"Explain."

"They got jobs as bouncers in some fancy club downtown. A big fight broke out, and instead of just tossing people, they...messed everybody up really badly. One of them—Yuri, I think—picked a guy up and spiked him head-first on concrete. Guy's a quadriplegic now."

"You were there?"

"No, but Mr. John was. He saw everything. He also saw to the brothers getting off on some bullshit self-defense thing. Apparently more than a few on the jury were faithful clients to Mr. John. How he managed that, I'll never know."

"And so these guys—the brothers—they've been with Mr. John ever since?"

She nodded.

I stood and began pacing. I felt like I needed to piss and shit and puke.

"What's wrong?" she said.

"Seriously? After what you just told me, you're asking me what's wrong?"

"You dealt with a monster like Gene okay."

"Gene was just a musclebound lump—and he *still* almost killed me. If it wasn't for that pervert with the camera being a distraction I'd be shark shit right now. And I'll tell you something else: good grapplers are a fucking *nightmare* in a real fight. You don't sneak in that first punch—and make it fucking count—and they'll have you on your back faster than a sneeze. Anyone who says otherwise simply hasn't fought one—period. Oh and here's another newsflash for you: my grappling *sucks* ."

She held up a placating hand. "Okay, fine. It's all irrelevant anyway—if you do this right, you're not going to have to fight anyone."

"How's that?"

"You'll have a gun."

"Won't *they* ?"

"You'll have the element of surprise on your side. They won't be expecting anyone."

"I've shot a gun twice in my entire life. I'm anything but a deadeye."

"They'll be drinking. They'll need to use the bathroom. You can hide out in the locker room and pick them off one at a time. Close range."

"And the aftermath? You're not gonna tell me that if I pull this off, I have to load them up and drive their bodies back to my buddy Manny, are you?"

"No. It'll be a get in, get out kind of thing."

"Just leave? Leave their bodies?"

"It'll be chalked up to a million things except the truth, Calvin. A robbery, drugs, a grudge…"

"Grudge? Thought no one knew who this guy was?"

"Mr. John might be able to hide his true identity from most, but he doesn't hide his wealth. Exceptional wealth always comes at the expense of others. I'd wager digging into grudges would be the very first area of pursuit."

"A million things except the truth, huh? What *is* the truth?"

"That a massage therapist did it so he wouldn't have to star in snuff films anymore."

THE BAR

"So you believed her?" the bartender asks.

"At first? No. I figured she was up to something. Especially after she mentioned stealing his money after he was dead."

"But...?"

"But there were a lot of things that didn't make sense. Like she could have easily told Mr. John to go ahead and kill me—there are pathetic guys like me all over the world who would gladly fill my spot in order to appease a Goddess like Angela. But instead she lets him pull out her teeth in hopes that she *might* be able to convince me to stay? I mean for all she knew, I could have been halfway to Brazil when he was yanking out her choppers. Hell of a risk."

"What else?" he asks.

"Motive," I say, draining my scotch. "I couldn't figure out an ulterior motive."

"The money," he says. "You just said the money concerned you as an ulterior motive."

"True. But the more I thought about it, the more I wondered if it would be so bad—if she took the money and I never saw her again. At least Mr. John would be dead. Plus, I already admitted to you that a part of me contemplated eliminating the problem at the source which, at the time, was *her* . When that source changed from Angela to some psycho kingpin gunning for me, well, there wasn't much to contemplate anymore. It seemed a no-brainer."

"So you *did* end up believing her?"

I shake my head. "No—not a hundred percent. I still sensed something iffy. So I did a few things. First, I convinced myself that if I went through with her crazy plan, I'd be doing it for *me* ; not her. It was *my* freedom I was after.

"Second, I needed a way to test her supposed loyalty to me. True, the missing teeth were a pretty big passing grade, but I'm talking as far as the money was concerned. For all I knew, this Mr. John had a couple mill at that club, and what was a few missing teeth for a couple mill?—she could buy as many new teeth as she wanted afterwards. So I needed a way to test her loyalty when it came to the money."

"Which was?"

I hold up a *let me finish* -hand. "And third, I wasn't about to do a single fucking thing until one little detail was taken care of first. Again, another way of testing her supposed loyalty to me—except this one was *far* more important than money."

"What was it?" He looks the eager audience again. I'd caught him rolling his eyes a couple of times during the shark story (I can't blame him; even *I* can't believe that insanity really happened), but now he's back, eyes fixed, wanting more without judgment—at least for the moment. No doubt he still thinks I'm a crazy drunk, spinning a good yarn, but I've got him hooked again. So I give the hook a tug and guide him towards my now empty scotch glass. He fills it instantly. I'm drunk, but not so drunk as to veer and begin complaining how entitled kids are these days, or that the '86 Celtics could beat the '96 Bulls.

So I just grin at him, grant him no immediate gratification, and carry on at my own pace...

41

Angela and I went over her proposal a number of times, me leaking constant skepticism, she a constant optimism; that what she was proposing was *not* suicide.

The concept remained fairly straightforward: enter; kill bad guys; grab money; leave; yay freedom. Unfortunately, like most basic concepts, there were those pesky *what ifs?* that continuously swarmed in front of me like a bastard cloud of gnats.

What if I shoot and miss; they shoot and don't? What if they somehow see me coming and get the jump on me? What if it does come down to a fight and I'm left facing two guys who sound capable of bitch-slapping grizzly bears?

What if Angela was setting me up?

For what though?

(The money.)

Okay, yeah—the money. But does that even make sense? If it's all about the money, then why use me? I'm no Jason Bourne. Talk about low odds.

(Like she said; two birds…except maybe one of those birds is a ringer, has different priorities.)

You mean money before *freedom?*

(Why not? Maybe that's the genius of it; she figures she's got nothing to lose. If you carry out the plan, she gets money and freedom. If you die, she throws up her hands and feigns ignorance to Mr. John: "I don't know what he was doing there. As far as I knew, I'd convinced him to stay on board. Must have gotten some kind of vigilante nonsense in his head. Oh well.")

No, that can't be it. Angela could feign ignorance all she wanted; it would never explain how I knew they'd be at that club, how I'd gotten hold of a key.

(Maybe you tortured her in order to get it. Maybe you pulled out her teeth.)

What???

(Maybe Mr. John didn't threaten to kill you right away. Maybe he tells Angela she has a week to convince you and never lays a finger on her. Angela knows where he keeps his money, wants it, and the prospect of a dickhead like Mr. John dying in the

process is nothing short of a delightful bonus. So she yanks her own teeth and comes to you as the victim with a warning. The story she relays is all true except *the part about Mr. John wanting you dead without pause, and of course, Angela sacrificing her choppers in order to spare you. This builds a sense of trust. Maybe in reality, her disfiguration is more than just a trust-builder. Perhaps it doubles as a failsafe in case you fuck up at the club: "I didn't want to give him the key, Mr. John, but he tortured me. Look what he did to my teeth . . . ")*

That's insane.

(It's a theory.)

Maybe there really isn't one—an ulterior motive I mean. Maybe it's all exactly as she says it is. We keep on analyzing like this and we'll find a million different conspiracies, each more farfetched than the last.

Except the truth was, no matter how many conspiracies pin-balled inside my head about Angela's motives, the one immovable truth was that in a way, Angela's motives were ultimately irrelevant. *My* motives were paramount here: I had to do this or I was dead. The end. Were their other ways to this end? Better ways? Maybe—but I'll be damned if I knew what they were. Angela was my only source of information when it came to Mr. John, and chances were solid she had weighed every conceivable option that could be carried out during the week's stay of execution we'd been granted by his unholiness. After all, she wanted him dead just as much as I did—didn't she?

* * *

Before anything was to be even remotely started, I needed to make arrangements for Pele, and then say some goodbyes. *Final* goodbyes, you ask? Was I *expecting* to die tonight? I guess. It didn't mean I was accepting my fate and embracing death or any Zen shit like that. Oh no; I wanted to live, and I wanted to shoot all three of them in the face until the gun clicked empty. But I was no fool. I knew

(do you?)

the task that lay ahead. I knew the odds. I also knew that for the first time in as long as I can remember, I was living in the moment; not numb anymore. I guess I should be grateful—I'd finally gotten what I wanted.

I am a depressed, confused young man who is likely an alcoholic. I want to drink. Always. It is an *easier* means for living in the now. It allows you to stay in that safeguarded perimeter of your mind where the only true fear you have is the hangover to come the next day. It allows the beer-guzzling redneck screaming at his TV to think he can kick the shit out of the two boxers slugging it out for his entertainment. Allows him his very own safeguarded perimeter, one that acquires more spotlights and towers and snipers and barbed-wire fences with each new drink. And with each new drink comes that blessed acquisition of more assuredness. Because now that redneck goddamn *knows* he can whoop those two boxers slugging it out. Both at the same fucking time! And maybe someday, someone will call his bluff and put him in that ring, and he'll find himself fucked. Like me. I'm in the ring and I'm fucked. And now I must go and bid my farewells, and then prepare to be fucked hard.

42

My mother answered on the first ring.

"Hey, Mom."

"What's wrong?"

Any guesses as to where my pessimism comes from?

"Nothing's wrong. How are you?"

"I'm fine. I just ate some stew. I made a lot if you want to come get some and take it home with you."

That thought comforted me for some reason.

"Maybe I will thanks. Mom, do you think you can do me a favor and watch Pele for a few days?"

"Why?"

I wasn't going to use a going out of town line as it would raise too many questions. I kept it simple.

"I'm getting my apartment bugged for fleas. They're setting off one of those bomb things."

"Your cat has fleas? I don't want him if he has fleas."

"No, he doesn't have fleas, Mom. It's just a precautionary thing."

She sighed. "Okay."

"What's the matter? I thought you liked my cat."

"I do, I do. You can drop him by today. I can give you your stew then."

"What time?"

"Whenever. I'll be home."

"Okay—I'll be over soon. Thanks, Mom."

She said goodbye and hung up.

* * *

I headed towards my mother's house. It wasn't too dark outside just yet, but it was getting there. My mother didn't live far, but when you have an alpha cat like Pele caged in the back seat, howling loud enough to frighten wolves, distance can become a subjective thing indeed.

"We're almost there, brother," I said, reaching in back and poking my fingers through his carrier to scratch his head. I expected a swipe or a bite in retaliation for my audacity to cage him like some kind of animal, but instead he let me scratch him; even stopped his incessant howling, perhaps knowing in that inexplicable pet-way that our moments together might be numbered.

That thought didn't help at all, and I almost lost it right there.

* * *

My mother lived in a small, detached house in a quiet suburb. I pulled into her driveway and let myself out first before grabbing Pele. I stopped and allowed myself to breathe in the solitude of the neighborhood. It was so quiet it appeared suspicious. I thought about what Angela had said about Mr. John and that the reason he was so hard to get to was because no one knew who he was. I wondered how many Mr. Johns lived here. How many walked to the end of their drive every morning to fetch the paper, wearing a housecoat and carrying a cup of coffee, seemingly as innocuous as the next man? How many played golf together on weekends? Tended to their lawns? Fixed fences; washed cars; cleaned gutters; et cetera, et cetera? How many Mr. Johns were here, doing all of those things, the *real* truth buried beneath suburban ritual?

"Calvin? Are you coming in?"

My daze broke, and I turned towards my mother. She stood on her front step, one hand gripping both lapels of her light blue house robe by the neck, the other keeping the front door open.

"Hey, Mom. Let me get Pele and I'll be right there."

* * *

My mother's house smelled like lemons. It would not have surprised me if she began cleaning the second we got off the phone. Although my relationship with my mother was more routine than need, she still made a fuss for me. I suppose it was because my mother lived her entire life by a set of rules. She followed these rules regardless of her true feelings towards anyone or anything, and cleanliness for *any* visitor was a rule. The lemon smell was probably some kind of polish.

In case you couldn't tell from the endearing phone call we'd had earlier, my mother and I were not very close on an emotional level. I never sensed genuine warmth from her in all my twenty-nine years, but I'd be lying if I said she wasn't reliable. She was. Again, she lived by a set of rules, and another one of those rules was that she catered to her children regardless. She was not a mean woman, nor was she a pleasant woman. I can only remember her smiling a few times in my life, and they were when she was watching television.

Her relationship with my dad was pretty much the same as it was with her kids. She knew my dad was fucking everything and everyone with a heartbeat, but again, whether she cared or not was irrelevant. Her job was to be his wife. Those were the rules. My dad was a piece of shit, but he never beat her or beat us or anything. Hell, the guy was never home long enough to do so. I would wager good money the guy had a mistress in every state in America, and even a handful abroad. When he *was* home, you had to wonder why he even bothered. He would isolate himself in his study, come out for a family dinner that was always eaten in silence—I truly cannot remember a single conversation had between our family at the dinner table—then back to his study with a bottle of scotch, only to be seen the next night for dinner, if he wasn't heading out of town, of course.

My older sister got the same treatment from my mother, but like my father, she wasn't home often. Even as a teen she was at one friend's or another's most nights. This was fine by me as my relationship with her seemed exactly as expected in our household: grunts hello as we passed one another in the hallway.

If I could use an analogy that lacks creativity, you could say it was like living with a family of robots. They performed as they were programmed to do, but lacked the heart to bring a family close together. I'm not trying to make myself out to be a victim of the classic dysfunctional family. *I* certainly made no effort to make any changes within the robot circle. Even if I wanted to, I wouldn't have known how. I can remember being at friend's houses over the years, hanging out with their families. It used to genuinely creep me out when they laughed and joked at the kitchen table, or actually sat with one another in the den and talked out of want instead of obligation. As void as my family was, I was sure I didn't want what my friends had either. There was a sort of freedom in my family; you could come and go as you pleased. This was both a good thing and a bad thing. Good because, well, the freedom; bad because I had no structure. I had no goals and no drives. I was never taught how to pursue, nor was I taught how to give up and blame. I was just taught how to be.

"He looks big," my mother said, looking inside Pele's pet carrier.

I joined her and looked inside the carrier by lifting it to eye level. It took two arms; Pele weighed a ton. He also looked very pissed off.

"When was the last time you saw him?" I asked.

She shrugged. "I don't know. A year?"

I set the carrier down and went in for a hug. She obliged me, but kept her eyes on the carrier. "You sure he doesn't have fleas?"

I pulled away. "No, Mom, I promise."

I bent and let Pele out of his carrier. He exited and started slinking as low to the carpet as possible while keeping his nose high and alert for any potential threats nearby. I could actually hear him sniffing anything and everything.

"You've still got his litter box?" I asked.

She nodded. "Just filled it. It's in the downstairs bathroom."

"Great. I'm gonna show him where it is. He's a good cat—I'll show him once and he'll be fine."

"I'll be in the kitchen."

* * *

I sat at the kitchen table, my mother busying herself behind me.

"Do you want some stew?" she asked.

Ah, I had forgotten about the stew. Whoever programmed my robot of a mother installed an exceptional cooking program inside her. I'm actually surprised I did not look to food as my savior during childhood and balloon to eight hundred pounds.

"That would be great, Mom. Thanks."

A little more shuffling behind me and soon a hot bowl of stew was my reward. She placed it on the table before me, followed by a glass of water. Ever since my father died, there had never been so much as a drop of alcohol in the house.

I took a bite as she joined me at the table. "Mmm...it's good, Mom."

She nodded a thank you. "How's work? Are you still massaging?"

"Yeah."

"Are you seeing anyone?"

I thought of Angela, her beauty, the sex. And then before I could help it, my mind showed me the rest: the freak, Stephanie, the fucking shark.

Looking down at my bowl I muttered, "No, not really."

My mother reached across the table and patted my hand. "You'll find someone."

I faked a smile. "What about you? You seeing anyone?"

She made the sign of the cross on her chest. She was the only one in the family whoever went to church. "Calvin, your father is gone."

I swallowed a bite of stew. "So?"

She frowned a little. "So my husband has passed on."

"Yeah but you haven't."

"Oh, stop it, Calvin."

"Well, Christ, Mom, it wasn't like he was a poster boy for monogamy."

Now she frowned a lot. " *I beg your pardon?* "

I looked down at my bowl again. "Sorry, Mom. I just worry about you being on your own, you know?"

"I have you and your sister to check in on me," she said.

I snorted. "And when was the last time *she* dropped by?"

My mother didn't answer, just closed her eyes and turned her head as if I'd said nothing, as if my sister wasn't a woman who placed substance abuse—

(*HA!*)

—and promiscuity above all else.

I tried denting her armor of denial anyway. "I'm just saying, what if I wasn't around anymore, Mom? What if something happened to me?"

She made the sign of the cross again. "God forbid."

I sighed and gave up. Took a final bite of stew, pushed back my chair and stood. "Okay—well I better get going."

She followed me into the foyer. "Do you want to take some stew home with you?"

"I'm not going home, remember?"

"Oh right. Where are you staying while your house is being bombed?"

"Paul's."

"You know you're welcome to stay here."

I gave her another fake smile. "Thanks, Mom. Paul's expecting me though."

I started calling for Pele.

"How long will I have to look after him?" she asked.

Pele appeared and made a beeline for me, circling and rubbing against my shins. *We've stayed long enough. Take me home.*

"Not sure yet," I said. "Hoping it's not long."

I bent and picked him up. He began purring immediately. I hugged him and kissed the top of his head a few times. He usually didn't mind being held, but he hated being kissed. He allowed it now, and I felt my throat swell and my eyes fill. "You'll take good care of him, right?" I managed, my voice nearly cracking.

"Of course I will."

I hugged and kissed Pele again. "I love you, buddy. Be good." I set him down, turned and hugged my mother without warning. The tears in my eyes were stronger now. "I love you, Mom."

She seemed stunned by my sudden—and heartfelt—embrace. But before long she was hugging me back with equal affection. "I love you too, sweetheart." She pulled away from the hug and grabbed me by the shoulders, studying me. "Are you okay, Calvin?"

I smiled—a real one this time—and wiped a tear away with the back of my hand. "I'm fine."

"I'll see you soon?"

"I hope so."

43

All things considered, goodbyes with my mother and Pele had gone about as well as they could have. Paul, on the other hand, was going to take some finagling. He'd had no problem voicing his suspicions about my behavior as of late, and to be truthful, I wasn't even sure I should call him. What could I possibly say without raising his suspicions even higher? There was a desperate part of me that wanted to tell him everything. He was my best friend and I loved him more than anyone alive. But I knew Paul; if I told him, he would insist on some kind of involvement, assuming he didn't tell me I was nuts for going through with this craziness first—which he assuredly would.

I couldn't tell him. No way. Like the night at the bar where I hacked into my calf to remind me to keep my mouth shut, I needed to be just as disciplined here—more so. If I'd slipped up at the bar, my punishment would have only been a barrage of questions followed by a barrage of rhetorical questions, asking if I used to take the short bus to school. If I slipped up now? Told him everything? I don't even want to *think* about my punishment. As I said, Paul—after telling me I was a fucking idiot—would insist on some kind of involvement. If something happened to me, so be it. If something happened to me *and* Paul? Christ, I got sick just thinking about it.

I pulled into the parking lot of the Winchester Hotel. It was the nicest place with the closest proximity to the club. Angela had selected it, and she was inside, waiting for me. I was a few minutes early—as I'd planned—and I used that opportunity to call Paul. I dialed his cell, and was still unsure as to what I was going to say, even after the third ring. His voicemail eventually came on, and a part of me felt relief—it would be better to leave a message than to suffer his questioning.

"Hey, man, it's me. I'm just calling to apologize for my weird behavior lately. I'm actually sitting outside the Winchester Hotel right now. I'm about to go inside to meet this girl I've been kinda seeing lately. Unfortunately, I'm not going in there to do what you think I'm going in there to do." I paused a second and took a breath that felt like smog down my lungs. "I got into some serious shit, man...and there's a good chance I'm not gonna..." I cleared my throat. "If I don't see you again..."

Don't cry don't cry don't cry don't cry

"...I just need you to know how lucky I am to have a friend like you. I love you, man."

I hung up, turned off my phone, and cried.

44

I stood outside the hotel room. I did not knock. Just stood there, my nose six inches from the peep hole. I thought about turning and leaving. I thought about option B—running. Could I live the rest of my life running in fear? Could I live with Angela's death on my conscience if Mr. John did end up hanging her on that meat hook? I kept telling myself I was doing it for me, to save my own life, and I was, but it was becoming more and more real by the second, my body struggling to adjust to the side effects of this new drug reality. And the irony of it all was anything but amusing. No more numb? Living in the now? We've got just the pill, sir. Side effects may include extreme doubt, paranoia, and scared shitlessness.

I raised a fist to knock, froze, and then lowered my hand.

If I run, he'll find me, right?

(Maybe.)

If I do this, I could die. If I don't do it, I'll definitely die.

(If they find you.)

Why wouldn't they? I'm no survivalist who can live off the grid. I'd have no clue where to even begin.

(Then we don't have a choice, do we?)

No. This IS the safer of the two options. This way I've got the element of surprise; like Angela said. If I run, I'm handing that element over to them.

(Then knock. Take the first step and knock.)

I raised my fist and knocked.

Angela immediately opened the door. If I didn't know any better, I would have thought she was watching me through the peep hole, studying my apprehension.

As soon as she let me in, she closed the door, locked it, and gave me a powerful hug. "Thank you," she said.

I pulled away and held her at arms' length. "I'm doing this for us you know. You *and* me."

She nodded. "I know that." Her front teeth were still gone.

"It's just like you said: I'm saving *our* asses."

She gave another nod.

I took a deep breath, held it for a second, then let it out slow. "Okay then…what do you have for me?"

She pointed to a black leather bag on the bed. It looked like the kind of bag a doctor who made house calls would carry.

"What's in there?" I asked.

"Hopefully everything you'll need."

I opened the bag. Inside were a gun and an impressive looking knife. I held up the knife. "What's this for?"

She gave a partial shrug. "I don't know. Just in case?"

I wagged the knife at her like a finger. "If I lose the gun, they're going to use this to check my prostate."

"Stop it."

I put the knife back in the bag and took out the gun. I saw an emblem that read Glock near the gun barrel. A long dark cylinder that looked like a piece of pipe was attached to the barrel. I'm no gun guy, but I'd seen enough movies to guess that dark cylinder attached to the barrel was a silencer. I asked anyway, tapping the end of the weapon with my finger. "This a silencer thingy?"

"Yeah. Don't ask where I got it."

I wasn't about to. For all I knew it was hers—one of many.

I put the gun back in the bag. "What about the key?"

She went into her pocket and produced a thick brass key. "This will get you in the back door. I'd park a good distance away, then make the remainder on foot. A car in the back lot after hours might raise suspicion." She handed me the key. "You feel good about the floor plans?"

"I think so." I then studied her carefully after asking: "Still no idea about the money?"

"It'll be there. *Where?* is the question. You might have to…" She gave a partial shrug.

"What?"

"Get him to show you."

"I imagine he'll be eager."

"So you make him eager," she said.

I snorted and shook my head. "You really do think I'm James Bond."

"So…" she said, ignoring my doubt. "They should be there by now. Probably into their first bottle of vodka already. Now's as good a time as any."

"No—not yet it's not." I sat down on the bed. "I need one last thing from you before I go *anywhere* ."

45

"What one last thing?" she said.

"I want the tape."

"What tape?"

"The one with you, me, and the freak, Angela. The one where I was bound— *by you* —and then attacked by some bat-wielding psychopath—at *your* command—forcing me to *defend* myself. Not that edited nonsense that makes me look like Jason fucking Voorhees. I want the *original* ."

She stared back at me with a good poker face. I'm not sure what kind of reaction I expected—maybe I wanted to rattle her a little—but I did not expect her to look as composed as she did. Perhaps she'd been expecting it, wondered why it took me so long to mention the damn thing.

"I want that tape," I said again. "I'm putting my life on the line here tonight, and if I live, I want proof that I was, in fact, acting in self-defense should any of Mr. John's friends decide to send that edited bullshit into the wrong hands."

"It's a DVD," she said.

"Huh?"

"Nobody uses tapes, Calvin."

"Are you honestly trying to divert with this semantic bullshit?"

"No—I was just saying."

"I don't care what kind of fucking *format* you use, I want the footage. The *original* footage."

"How do you know I still have it?"

"What?"

"How do you know I didn't destroy the original?"

Shit—I'd never considered that. For the very life of me, I don't know why, but I'd never considered that. Whatever leverage I thought I'd achieved in this exchange was now gone. I could try and bluff, try some kind of psychology about her being the narcissistic type who would prefer to hold on to the original as a reminder of her prowess in all things manipulation, a sociopath who keeps trophies of past conquests. But I no longer believed Angela was a sociopath. I didn't even believe she was a narcissist. Any bluff on my part would have been transparent to an eye as sharpened as hers. So I said the only thing I could manage:

"Did you?"

She paused a moment, looking down at me. "No," she eventually said. "I still have it."

And then, instead of asking for it once more, I asked something else. "Why?"

She sighed. "Maybe I kept it for the same reason you want it."

"To prove my innocence?"

"Maybe—if it ever came to that."

(*Do you believe her? Do you believe her??*)

"I'd still like to have it," I said. "For peace of mind, if nothing else."

"It'll be waiting for you when you get back."

"I see—I come back alive, and my reward is the uncut version of Calvin and The Freak."

She ignored my shot at levity and said: "And me—if you want me."

My cynicism, momentarily humbled during Angela's reasoning for not destroying the original film, suddenly resurfaced from its pool of self-preservation. "Don't forget about the money. Can't forget about that, right?"

She sighed. "Yeah…and the money."

THE BAR

"I know that place," the bartender says. "That spa club. You're talking about the one on Beck Street, right? Long, one-story building? Kinda hidden behind a shopping center?"

I nod.

"Yeah—I've actually been there. A buddy of mine had guest passes. Place is unreal. Like one of those Greek bath houses you see in books and movies. Fancy tile, marble columns, fountains. I tell ya; if I had the money…"

I sip my scotch and say nothing.

"So wait—" He pauses, something hitting him, yet seemingly unsure how to phrase it. "The spa club…"

"Yeah?"

"Your face, the money you keep laying on the bar…"

I only stare at him.

"You did it," he says. "You pulled it off."

I look away, replaying it all in my head. Despite the fuzzy clarity the alcohol has given the film, the ending is always the same.

Angela.

I drain my scotch and wince, but not from the scotch. "I didn't pull off shit."

PART NINE

MR. JOHN

46

The club was on Beck Street, tucked away behind a haughty shopping center that sported a Whole Foods instead of an Acme, gourmet coffee bars instead of proper bars. The club's modest locale seemed intentional; advertising was word of mouth. The extravagant architecture a monetary deterrent to those who happened by.

A solitary car was in the club's lot. A black Mercedes with tinted windows.

(Angela drives a black Mercedes with tinted windows.)

Maybe it was Mr. John's?

(Or maybe she's inside.)

What sense would that make?

(Has ANY of this shit made sense so far?)

I continued past the club for about fifty yards, pulled a U-y, rolled alongside the curb until I had a good view of the club from afar, and killed the engine. The key Angela had given me was to gain access through the back of the club. That meant the rest of the way would have to be done on foot—a car in the back lot after hours would raise too much suspicion, she'd said.

I glanced over at the passenger seat. The black leather bag was there, as ominous as ever. I opened it, took out the gun. I'd held it once since Angela had given it to me. It felt unnatural then, and it felt just as unnatural now. More so.

(Sure does beat a baseball bat or a machete though.)

I put the gun back in the bag and exited my car.

47

For the second time in my life, I stood outside a locked door, holding the key, my objective to enter and kill someone.

No mask this time. Masks were only if you'd planned on leaving people alive—or were being filmed. None of that applied here.

The second time in my life. I'd wager two percent of the population had done it *once* . And I'm discounting military and law enforcement, of course. Hopefully I needn't explain why. *Maybe* I'd get a few justice points for offing scumbags like Mr. John and his help, but any I'd earn would bounce off the mountain of debt I'd accrued after the Stephanie incident.

Second time in my life. I looked down at the black leather bag in my hand. No box-cutter in there. We got us a Glock and a foot-long knife that could shave a beard of nails.

I opened my fist and looked at the brass key. Angela's words in my head: *"This gets you in. You feel good about the floor plans? The money will be there. Where? is the question. You might have to...get him to show you... They should be there by now. Probably into their first bottle of vodka already. Now is as good a time as any..."*

They were here already. On the other side of this door. Not a drugged woman. Three men,

(and maybe Angela?)

two of them lethal.

Angela's words in my head again: *"I'll be waiting for you when you get back."*

I used the key and went inside.

48

The lighting was poor, the smell of chlorine immediate. I took a few steps forward, each step as if I feared the ground might crumble beneath me. Two more steps, and then I paused to listen. I heard nothing significant, just the constant hum of motors I presumed to be running the tubs and fountains of the place. Not that I could see them just yet—I was still too deep in back, still surrounded by the club's utilitarian design, reserved for employee eyes only.

A few more delicate steps and I heard something. People talking in the distance. My heart began a rapid beat that instantly found its way to my ears. I held my breath to compensate, but the drumming of my pulse would not be deterred. I needed to get closer.

My steps forward were light and calculated, the floor beneath me changing from ceramic to marble tile. The smell of chlorine grew stronger, the humidity increasing and forming a faint mist. I was approaching the hot tubs. So far, the layout Angela had given me had proved correct. The hot tubs were at the far end of the club, swimming pools and other amenities in front. She'd said Mr. John and his protection would be in the hot tubs, drinking. I'd told her I was crap with a gun. She'd said to hide in the locker room and pick them off one by one when they inevitably went in to take a leak.

I continued further, two, maybe three more steps max. The mist was getting stronger, its veil forcing me to squint. I remained tight to the wall, the corridor providing me good cover from the voices bathing in the wide-open luxuries ahead. I could see the locker room door—half a dozen feet ahead and to the left. I could manage those half a dozen feet and slip inside while still maintaining good cover. So far, Angela was steering me just fine.

I made the half a dozen steps. The mist increased, but so did the voices. My pulse still thumped my head, but proximity was now my ally. I held my breath again. I could hear them. The bass of male voices.

(Any female?)

I craned my neck forward, thought about risking a few more steps forward for a quick peek, but self-preservation kept me rooted. I held my breath once again.

Still the heavy bass of male voices.

No—I don't hear a female.

(Don't you look.)

I won't.

(Don't)

I won't!

An accent on one of the male voices. It sounded Russian.

She's right again. So far, everything Angela's said has been right. (*Then get in that fucking locker room and get ready to finish this.*)

Firm grip on the leather bag, I crept over towards the locker room door, eased it open, and slipped inside. I waited a tick, ear pressed to the door, making sure I hadn't been spotted or made a noise that needed investigating. I heard nothing but the steady bass of their chatter, no change in tempo, no cause for alarm. I let out a long sigh, turned and began searching for the bathroom stalls. I would lay in wait in one of those stalls like a trapdoor spider.

The stalls weren't a difficult find. The restroom area was adjacent to the communal showers, a strip of wall dividing them. On the left you had your sinks, your urinals, your stalls. On your right you had your beautifully tiled communal shower with multiple high-powered showerheads in a row; and beneath one of those showerheads, you had your giant naked man covered in tattoos, standing there with his back to you, getting ready to take a shower.

49

Straight ahead, a good ten feet away, was a monster of a man, more ink than pink covering his entire body—yes, his entire body. The guy was ass-naked, back to me, and in the process of hanging a large white towel onto one of the hooks to the right of the showerhead. He had not seen or heard me enter. My presence alone felt loud enough to turn him, but thankfully he now seemed fixated on adjusting the levers on the shower to an agreeable temperature. Still, I had seconds before he turned and saw me. I could open the leather bag now, snatch the gun, and shoot him in the back. *Boom* —one down. I would then hide in the stalls to the left of the showers and wait like the trapdoor spider. Yes.

I went to open the bag.

The bang of the locker room door swinging open froze me. No subtle entry like mine. Drunk and in need of a piss.

I spun in panic to meet the new offender…momentarily forgetting about the naked offender behind me.

" *Ahueyet!?* " I heard the naked offender behind me yell, a split-second before he knocked me out.

50

" *Whoosee?* "
    " *Idono.* "
    " *Whoosafuckisee?* "
    " *Idonfuckino.* "
It felt like I was underwater.
    "Whosafuckisee?"
    "Idonfuckino."
And then I began floating upwards, like the anchor had been cut, the surface clarity my reward.

"So who the fuck is he?" Annoyed American voice.

"I don't fucking know." Annoyed Russian voice.

"What the *fuck* is he doing here?" Annoyed American.

"I *don't know* ." Annoyed Russian.

Shuffling around me, followed by angry American saying: "Get him up. Get him on his feet."

I was snatched by the hair and belt and yanked to my feet, then backwards into the lockers with a metallic bang, a forearm pressed into my throat and staying there. Things were still fuzzy, but the haze was fading quickly.

I was in the locker room. I've made a colossal fuck up of the entire plan, and I'm looking at three pissed off gentlemen who I'd assume are Mr. John, Yuri, and Vlad.

Mr. John was wearing a white undershirt and boxer shorts. Probably the first thing he grabbed after hearing the commotion in the locker room. He's about average height, dark hair and eyes, handsome-ish. He truly *did* look like your average American Joe that could be your neighbor.

His Russian buddies did not. Yuri and Vlad would be cul-de-sac chatter the second the U-Haul arrived. Both bald, both frowning lumps of muscle, both with eyes cold and gray. The one with the tattoos had since (thankfully) slipped on his swim trunks, but remained shirtless. The other was dressed the same; shirtless and swim trunks.

Mr. John was seated on a bench, my gun in his hands, the knife lying next to him.

"So who is he?" Mr. John asked.

Both brothers said nothing.

"So who are you?" Mr. John asked me.

I squirmed to relieve some pressure from Vlad or Yuri's tattooed forearm against my throat. "You know who I am," I managed.

His eyebrows went up. "Do I? Well please enlighten me. Because I must say, I haven't the slightest clue."

I squirmed some more; it felt like a baseball bat was being pressed into my neck.

"Vlad?" Mr. John said patiently. "If he passes out, I won't get my answers."

So tattoo was Vlad. He lightened the pressure—a little.

"I work for you," I eventually said.

"A disgruntled employee?" He smiled. "I have many people working for me. What makes you so special?"

"I'm not," I said.

"Oh, I can see that. Still, I need to know why an insignificant such as yourself would risk coming in here, after hours, to attack an innocent businessman and his two associates. Were you after a raise or something?"

His comment made Vlad chuckle. Yuri stood in the background, scowling, arms folded.

"Businessman?" I said. "You're a sick fuck."

Forearm still on my throat, Vlad looked over his shoulder to gauge his boss' reaction to my comment. Mr. John did not look upset. He merely shrugged his shoulders and started nodding.

"I see," he said, still nodding. "Well...you must be a pretty tough guy to come in here all by yourself." Addressing Vlad and Yuri now: "What do you guys think? He look tough to you?"

Yuri and Vlad said nothing.

"Well come on, boys—this is what I pay you for. Can I please find out how tough this guy is?"

51

Vlad took his forearm off my throat and took a step back. I bent over and started coughing, pretending my breathing had suffered more than it had. A possum at play if there ever was one. The element of surprise would add to the effectiveness of my shot; as the old—and very apt—saying goes: it's the punch you don't see that knocks you out. Once Vlad was asleep, I'd continue nurturing that element of surprise and start cracking every fucking thing that moved. My only hope was that I put Yuri out before Mr. John remembered he was holding my gun.

I coughed some more, still bent over.

Vlad flicked the top of my head. "Cough, cough, little baby."

I launched myself upward, my right fist rocketing towards his jaw with every ounce of juice I had...

...And Vlad parried it easily, countering with his own right, shattering my nose. I dropped to all fours, my nose—or what was left of it—a bloody faucet.

" *Oooohh...* " Mr. John said. "How you doing, tough guy?"

I cupped a handful of the blood pouring from my nose and flung it towards Mr. John.

Vlad immediately ripped me to my feet by the hair and fired three sledgehammer uppercuts into my body. I dropped to all fours again and puked up my Mom's stew.

I heard Mr. John laugh, and I was pretty sure Yuri and Vlad started laughing too.

"What the hell?" I eventually managed, squinting upward as though looking into the sun, "I thought you were a grappler..."

" *You want grapple!?* " With a sudden burst, Vlad ripped me to my feet yet again, ducked then snaked his free arm between my legs, and hoisted me up and onto his shoulders in a classic firemen's carry. I wiggled and fought to no avail; he was a fireman saving a child. I lay draped across his massive shoulders like a human scarf, waiting to be spiked head-first onto that hard tile floor, hoping I'd die on impact as opposed to becoming another notch on the brothers' quadriplegic post.

Of all people, it was Mr. John himself who saved me from becoming that notch. "Vlad…" he said calmly.

Vlad, still holding me, keener than ever to get to the spikin', gave a reluctant glance over his shoulder.

"Vlad, put him down and give Yuri a turn." Mr. John spoke as if they were his children. You've played with it enough now; give your brother a turn.

Vlad dropped me. Better than being slammed, but still no fun. I rolled to all fours yet again.

Yuri approached. "Get up."

I stayed put, surrounded by my own blood and vomit.

Yuri nudged me in the side with the toe of his foot. "I say get up."

"I say fuck your mother."

(*What!?*)

Yuri exploded downward with a pile-driving punch into my kidney. I cried out and rolled onto my side. The pain was so intense, I almost puked again.

"Kid's got balls, I'll give him that," Mr. John said.

Still on my side, still writhing and grimacing and clutching at a kidney I feel has burst, I for some reason asked: "You wanna borrow them?"

A brief pause. And then finally a little chuckle. "You know, that's not such a bad idea," Mr. John said, setting the gun aside and then picking up the knife.

(*You FUCKING idiot…*)

And the male ego's foresight remains forever blind.

52

Mr. John tossed Yuri the knife. He caught it by the handle, squatted and started waving it in front of my face, grinning. "I take one first, or both at same time?"

Obviously, I said nothing.

"I don't think he's listening," Mr. John said, now propped casually on his side by an elbow, the bench his sofa, my plight his film. New ground for him, I'm sure. "Can you please check and see if he's listening first?"

Yuri, still squatting in front of me, still grinning, gripped my left ear and sliced it clean-off.

The pain was awful, yet not as bad as the kidney or the broken nose. Huh. Still, I could not help but moan and place a hand over the new hole in my head.

Yuri wiggled my severed ear in front of my face. "Look what I haaaaave…"

All three of them laughed. Yuri tossed the ear and wiped his hand on me.

"Think he's listening now?" Mr. John said.

"Maybe we take the other?" Vlad said.

Yuri slapped me, then jerked my head so he could get to my remaining ear. He gripped it tight between his thumb and index finger.

"Are you forgetting his offer?" Mr. John said.

Yuri looked over his shoulder.

Mr. John gave a theatrical splay of the hands. "I have no balls, gentlemen. He's willing to lend me his."

Yuri grinned again. Traced the knife down my curled body until it arrived at my groin. Started tapping the blade against my hip, breaths of anticipation coming out that grinning mouth like he wanted to fuck me.

More laughter at my squirming.

"Pussy," I said. It was soft and labored, but they heard it.

The laughter stopped.

"Come again?" Mr. John said.

"I said pussy. You're a fucking pussy."

Yuri stood upright. Both he and Vlad looked at Mr. John; this was never in any of the scripts they'd read.

"Really?" Mr. John said. "We're pussies, are we?"

I inched on my side until my eyes met Mr. John's. I had no ear; my shattered nose was still a painful, leaky mess; and my entire body throbbed like a hangover. Yet I made sure when I locked eyes with this prick, he saw none of my pain, only a willful man stating an absolute fact. "No—not them. You. *You're* the pussy. *One…big…giant…pussy.* " I then rolled onto my back and started laughing. Light at first, and then loud and uncontrollable, like a lunatic.

Behind my tears, I could make out Yuri and Vlad still exchanging looks as if they'd been asked a riddle. Mr. John's expression was a far different read. He was livid. In one furious movement, he snatched the gun, leapt from the bench, and jammed the barrel in my face. Still laughing, I closed my eyes and waited to die.

It never came. Two loud knocks on the locker room door came instead.

53

Mr. John took the gun off me and whipped it toward the locker room door. No one breathed.

Two more knocks.

"Who is that?" Vlad said.

Mr. John said nothing. He inched toward the door, gun now held behind his back. Yuri went to follow but Mr. John held up a hand, stopping him.

Three knocks now.

"Who *is* that?" Vlad asked again.

Mr. John spun on his man. In a loud whisper: " *Shut up! Whoever the hell it is, we don't want them coming in here and seeing THIS.* " He waved an arm back and forth over my mangled body. " *Just shut up, and maybe they'll go away.* "

More knocking.

Mr. John cursed under his breath, tucked the gun into his shorts, pulled his undershirt over it, and headed towards the locker room door. He was a few feet away when he turned back to us.

To Yuri and Vlad: "Stay right there and don't make a sound."

To me: "You're still alive. You can stay that way. But if you make so much as a fucking fart, the three of us will pull an all-nighter taking you apart piece by piece. Up to you."

I said nothing.

Mr. John turned back to the door. Approached cautiously. Opened it a crack and poked his head out. "Hello?"

Nothing.

"Hello? Anyone there?"

Still nothing. He glanced back at us. "Stay here." He slipped through the crack and left.

All three of us stared at that door. Yuri and Vlad's thick chests heaved in anticipation, Yuri's a stark white, Vlad's a mural. My breath was no less anxious, my nose forcing me to breathe through my mouth.

Seconds passed. A minute. Nobody's eyes left the door.

"I don't like this," Yuri said. He began backing up towards the bathroom stalls.

Vlad glanced back at him. "Be quiet."

Yuri kept backing up. "Something is wrong."

" *Shut up!* It's nothing."

Yuri shook his head slowly, his gray eyes narrowing, one fist clenching and unclenching, the other forever clenched on the knife as if it were his lifeline. "No...prepare, brother."

Vlad spun, angry. " *Zatknis' na hui!*"

The locker room door opened. Paul entered wielding a gun. He fired two shots into Vlad's chest, launching him backwards into the showers, Vlad's dense, tattooed body hitting the tiled floor with a wet and heavy slap.

Paul's eyes, frantic and scared, then fell on me; and I looked up with eyes equally frantic and scared—and completely dumbfounded. Paul dropped to my side instantly and began checking me.

I pushed him off. I wanted him to leave. Yuri was still here, lying in wait—a *true* trapdoor spider. Even with a gun, Paul had no chance. My words came out all wrong though:

"There's still one more, man. Back there by the toilets. There's still one more," I said. It was a warning, not an order. But Paul sprang to his feet. He'd heard no warning; he'd heard an order to continue forward, to charge those stupid fucking toilets and eliminate the final threat.

" *Paul, wait!* "

Yuri appeared out of nowhere, snatching Paul's gun-hand by the wrist and forcing it skyward, Yuri's free hand, his knife-hand, driving up and into Paul's gut, the gun falling from Paul's hand and to the tile floor with a clatter, Yuri then jerking the long blade free, gripping a slumped Paul by the shoulders and tossing him aside as though he'd lost interest, Paul falling hard to the tile, eyes closed, blood painting his mouth and chin, his shirt already awash in wet red.

I will never forget these images.

What happened next was harder to recall. Rage has a way of muddling things.

I know that I was on my feet without realizing, diving for the discarded gun. Yuri dove too, the knife coming down with him, catching me in the shoulder, the blade hitting my scapula, scraping bone. The pain was like a drug; it made me energized and manic. I scrambled for the gun, Yuri on top of me, raising the knife again. My right hand reached the pistol and I managed to spin under his weight and face him. My sudden spin affected his aim; the blade came down and missed, hitting the tile inches from my face with a clank. I jammed the gun into Yuri's throat and pulled the trigger. His eyes went wide, and his mouth opened without words. He coughed blood and it sprayed my face. I bucked him off and he rolled onto his back, dropping the knife, clutching at his throat, eyes wider. Coughs of blood now sprayed his own face as they were expelled up, and then inevitably down.

I hurried to my feet, wiped blood from my face with the back of my forearm, and shot Yuri up and down his torso until those wide eyes never blinked again. Then a few steps over to Vlad, and a few more bullets into his chest, just to make sure.

Paul.

I dropped the gun and rushed to his side, adrenaline still anesthetizing my pain. His shirt was soaked in blood, his eyes still closed. I placed my good (only) ear to his face and listened. His breath was a shallow wheeze, but it was there.

I gripped his shoulder and shook him. "Paul... *Paul* ..."

He opened his eyes. "I'm here."

I felt like breaking down and sobbing right there. "What the fuck, man?"

He coughed. It had a wet, phlegmy gurgle to it that wasn't phlegm. "Did we get them all?"

I nodded. "They're all—" A sudden realization slapped me. "Mr. John. *Where's Mr. John?*"

"Who?"

" *The guy! The guy who went looking for you!* " I started to my feet. Paul grabbed my arm.

"It's okay, man...he's out...I knocked him the fuck out...how do you think I got the gun?"

"He's not dead?"

Another wet cough. "I don't know. I got him pretty good with my crowbar."

Paul kept a big crowbar with duct tape on the handle in his back seat. I used to tease him about it, calling him a wannabe tough guy and such. I couldn't be more grateful for the damn thing now. Still, Mr. John could be alive. Worse still, alive and awake.

I ran a hand over Paul's sweaty brow. "Stay here and hold on for me, brother, okay? Can you do that?"

More wet coughs. "Where the hell am I going?"

I got to my feet, spotted the gun by Vlad's corpse, snatched it, and hurried out the locker room door to find Mr. John.

54

To my delight, Mr. John was still asleep. Flat on his back by the hot tubs, eyes closed, mouth open. I saw Paul's crowbar lying next to him. I smiled, but only for a second. The crowbar's nostalgia for my friend brought with it a far more significant recall: Paul was hurt badly; I needed to hurry.

* * *

I kicked open the locker room door, dragging Mr. John along by the ankle. He was still fast asleep, head bumping and lolling lifelessly as I dragged him towards the toilets.

I glanced over at Paul. "Still with me, brother?"

He gave me a thumbs-up, but he was looking paler by the second.

(*Then save him. Stop this shit and get him the hell out of here.*)

I can't stop. I can't leave Mr. John alive and you know it. We've come this far. The hard part is done.

(*The hard part will be knowing you waited too long to save your friend.*)

Shut the FUCK up.

I dragged Mr. John to a urinal, grabbed him by the hair, and slammed his face into the porcelain mouth, my free hand on the silver handle, flushing repeatedly. He eventually stirred, then started to gasp and choke as the water flooded his nose and mouth. I kept him there a tick longer, then ripped his head free and tossed him away.

His wet face embellishing the look of a frightened child's, Mr. John scooted backwards on his ass, one hand out in front, pleading. "Whatever you want...whatever you want..."

"The money. Where is it?"

His frightened face shifted; he looked confused.

"The fucking money you bring here to make deposits! Where is it!?"

The confusion shifted back to fear. He stammered and fumbled his words. "I...it's in the front office...in the desk." And then a sudden look of self-reprimand. "I mean *under* the desk, it's *under* the desk."

"What do you mean?"

Another demonstrative face of self-reprimand, as though his earnest attempts might be taken into consideration come sentencing. "Sorry—it's on the underside of the *top drawer* . It's in a carrier belt attached to the *underside of the top drawer* . Take whatever you want…take it all."

"I will thanks." I kicked him in the face and sent him back to bed.

55

I sprinted out of the locker room and towards the front of the club. Found the front office with no trouble and literally ripped the top drawer free, spilling its contents everywhere. I turned the drawer over and sure enough, there was a canvas money belt attached underneath. A big one. The size of a snake that ate rats, not mice.

I pulled the belt free and unzipped it a few inches.

" *Fuck me...* "

Strike rats and replace with hundred dollar bills for that beautiful, beautiful snake's diet. And he'd been a hungry bugger. I pulled a stack—the paper money band that held it read $10,000—and fanned it beneath my nose to make sure it was real. I'm no banker or counterfeit specialist or whatever, but it smelled like real money to me. Looked like it too.

I put the stack back in the belt, zipped it up, slung it over my shoulder, and ran back to the locker room. Inside, I laid the belt next to Paul.

"What the hell's that?" he asked.

All I said was, "Almost home, brother," and started towards the toilets, plucking up the bloody knife next to Yuri's body en route.

Mr. John was still out. I bent and ripped off his undershirt. Then his boxers. He was now balls-naked—but not for long. I slapped him until he woke, his realization that he was naked hitting him like another slap as he cowered and cried and curled into a defensive ball.

I laughed. "You really are a pussy." I pulled the knife and he cried harder, curled tighter, retreating into himself his only means of defense. "I'd love to pull an all-nighter," I said, throwing his words back at him, "but I'm afraid I can't. So, I'm gonna have to make this count. Even though they're not much—looks like their roommate isn't much either—I'm going to take from you what you couldn't from me. Make sure you scream after, if you don't mind; I've always wondered if that whole high voice thing was a myth or not."

* * *

At Paul's side again. His eyes were closed. I called his name and he didn't respond. He was a ghostly white, his forehead now soaked with sweat, the lower half of his shirt no less soaked itself. How I wished it too was sweat.

I started to cry as I pulled him into my lap and cradled his head. "Come on, man, please wake up."

He opened his eyes.

"Paul? *Paul?* Can you hear me?"

"Where's your ear?"

I smiled, tears running down my bunched cheeks. "It's around here somewhere."

"You gonna tell me what this was all about?"

"I don't think now's the time, brother. We need to get you to a hospital."

"I'm fine."

"Like fun you are. You were stabbed with a fucking sword. We gotta go, man."

"I followed you."

"What?"

"I was being a petty little bitch…I screened your call. You've been weird lately, so I was ignoring you. But I listened to your message right after. I drove to the Winchester. You were still there. I followed you here…"

"Jesus, man…"

"So you gonna start explaining?"

"Not now. I don't want the cliché of you dying in my arms mid-sentence."

He chuckled, followed by a series of wet coughs. "Gotta say something…"

"Say whatever you want, brother, just please do it fast."

"My cock's bigger than yours."

"You don't want your last words to be a lie, do you?"

We both chuckled. And then we stopped.

"I love you, man," he said.

"That's not a cliché?" I said.

"Only if I died. I'm not gonna die."

"Fucking right you're not."

56

I pulled into the emergency strip at the nearest hospital and laid on the horn. I'd told Paul during the short drive that I would explain everything to him tomorrow, but only if he lived. He found that amusing and agreed to my suggestion, but only if I would sport the bill at Mick's once he was released. I agreed without pause.

"You should be checking in here with me," he said to me in the car, moments before he was carted away. "Look at you. Your fucking ear is gone. Your nose is the letter Z."

Two nurses hurried through the automatic doors, towards my car. Paul had a point. I looked like hell; it would warrant questioning. I couldn't allow that, at least not now. I had far too much to do.

"I need to take care of something first," I said, turning my profile to the approaching medical staff, grateful my right ear was still intact.

"Is this 'something' the reason where idling outside the ER?"

"Clever boy. Just sit tight and heal. I'll be back soon."

A nurse opened the passenger door. I told her Paul had been stabbed in a mugging. More staff approached, and Paul was soon taken away on a gurney. A nurse remained; keen to get more information from me. I mumbled something about coming right back, and then reached for the passenger door. She got a glimpse of my face—my broken nose, the two lovely black eyes that always accompany a good break—and asked if I was okay. I pulled the door shut and drove off without answering.

57

I hurried around my apartment, looking for the right spot. I settled on my laundry basket, a tall, deep hamper that was lucky to get emptied once a month. I flipped the lid and it was—no surprise—full. And that was good. Angela, or anyone else for that matter, would never go rooting in a dirty hamper, especially one as full as it was.

I stuffed the money belt deep, piled the dirty clothes on top, and closed the lid. I was satisfied. At least for now. Regardless of how things went with Angela, I wasn't planning on keeping the money there long.

I went to my bathroom next. I knew the mirror might be unkind, but didn't think it would be that cruel. I looked like a friggin' zombie. Ear gone, nose mashed, eyes black...

I winced as I lifted my shirt. My torso fit the costume. Black bruises the size of softballs (and why not, Vlad and Yuri's knuckles were the size of fucking softballs) were everywhere. I turned and looked over my shoulder. The mirror reflected the granddaddy softball of them all, covering one of my kidneys. I wondered if I had internal damage. My answer came a short moment later when I took a piss. All blood.

Back to my face. Nothing I could do for my nose except try like hell not to sneeze. My ear? Or lack thereof? Nothing I could really do for that either. Cover it I suppose so as not to freak people out, myself included. At the moment, it looked as if a quarter-sized wad of red Play-dough had been slapped over the hole. Ugly, but at least it had begun coagulating, stemming blood flow. I dug in my medicine cabinet and came upon a box of giant Band-Aids I don't remember buying, but they were there, and they were perfect for the job. I unwrapped one and placed it over the red wad of Play-dough.

I wanted to change clothes, for peace of mind, and, well, my current clothes had blood and vomit on them. Except if I changed clothes, Angela would know I stopped home before coming to see her. I didn't want that.

(*Then how do you explain the Band-Aid?*)

Ah, shit.

I winced as I pulled the Band-Aid off and tossed it in the trash. Fuck it; the gruesome sight would only add to Angela's shock—at least initially. Once I revealed certain "truths" it would be interesting to see if that initial shock swelled with sorrow, or shriveled with contempt.

Time to go find out.

58

I hurried past the reception desk at the Winchester Hotel and went right for the stairwell. I was fortunate the receptionist on duty was attending to someone else or I'm sure he would have called the police after getting a good look at me. I didn't even risk using the elevator for fear of sharing it with someone. So I climbed the stairwell, and eventually stood outside Angela's door for the second time this evening. First time, I can remember raising my fist, hesitant, knowing my knock would be the start of the snowball down the hill, the probability of my getting crushed under its accumulated weight at the bottom damn likely. This time...this time I didn't know what to think.

I knocked.

Angela opened the door and immediately placed a hand over her mouth. " *Oh my God...* " She leapt into my arms and I groaned in pain. She instantly backed off into the room and I followed, shutting the door behind me.

She approached cautiously now, hands out in front, wanting to touch, but pulling back every time as though she feared distorting me further. I saw her eyes lock on the hole where my left ear used to be. "Oh my God..." she said again. "What happened to your ear?"

"You mean other than the fact that it's gone?"

She put her hand to her mouth again. She looked like she might cry.

I walked past her and sat on the bed. "Yup...they got my ear and your teeth. All they need now is a nose and some eyes and they're in business."

She let out a simultaneous laugh and cry.

I sighed. "It's done though...it's all done."

She inched forward, still looking hesitant to touch me for fear of making things worse. "It's really done? They're gone?"

"They're gone."

She started crying. Sat next to me and started kissing me gently all over my broken face.

I pulled away.

She immediately apologized. "I'm sorry—does it hurt?"

"No, it's not that."

"What is it?"

"There was a problem."

"What do you mean?"

I paused, preparing to study her, hoping the expressions to follow would be a capable read; people like Angela are not breezy material.

"There was no money," I said.

"You couldn't find it?"

"It wasn't *there* . I tortured the fucking guy, Angela…there was no money."

She turned slowly away from me, seated on the corner of the bed now. I studied her body language intently; keen to read something, anything.

I saw her shoulders drop. Then her head. Then a hand on her brow followed by a sigh. Disappointment. Clear as day.

God damn it.

"I'm sorry," she said.

She was still turned away from me. I thought I heard her wrong.

"What?"

She turned and faced me again. The disappointment was there, but it did not share its expression with distaste or contempt as I'd feared. Nor did it share it with sorrow. Angela's disappointment, it would turn out, was rooted in shame. "You were counting on it, weren't you?" she said. "The money."

I opened my mouth then closed it. I had no reply.

"Calvin, I'm so sorry; I truly did believe it would be there." She placed a hand on my shoulder, an expression of hope trying to surface beneath the shame. "But it doesn't matter, okay? I told you, I have money. I have *a lot* of money. What I thought was at the club? That was just a perk. We don't need it…"

"You don't care about the money?" I asked.

" *No* . Why would I? All the money in the world wouldn't have been able to buy what you just gave me." She leaned in and kissed me on the cheek. "I'm indebted to you for the rest of my life."

"You don't care about the money," I said, not asked this time.

"I care that you came back to me." She kissed me a few more times and then pulled back, eyes going over my face. "I think we need to get you to a hospital."

I cupped a hand over the hole where my ear used to be. "Say that again?"

She gave a sympathetic little chuckle. "I'll drop you off at the ER. Then I'll go home and pack a few things. I want to stay with you when you get out."

"Sounds good to me." I then paused. "You won't forget to bring the tape will you?"

Her smile dropped. She appeared hurt for a short moment before eventually settling into a look of acquiescence. "That was the deal."

PART TEN

CASUALTIES

59

So Angela had passed my money test. Good. I'd figured it could have gone one of two ways: she got angry and took off, in which case, fuck you, and the money was all mine. Or, she'd do exactly as she'd done (exactly as I'd hoped) and told me she didn't care about the money, in which case, the only hurdle ahead was finding the right time and way to tell her I'd lied. I suspected she'd understand no matter when or how I told her though. It was a loyalty test after all, something I think she'd appreciate in retrospect—especially once I turned the money over and proclaimed it *ours* .

Getting a hold of that damn DVD was the big one though, where the *real* loyalty test lied. She'd proven herself sincere enough thus far, but until I had the uncut version of Calvin and The Freak in my hands, I would remain cagey. I had to.

* * *

The doctor told me what I already knew: my nose was badly broken. What I didn't know, was that it would need to be *re* -broken with the help of a plastic surgeon. As for my ear, it too could be repaired with the help of a plastic surgeon. Unfortunately, I would need to go to another hospital for such fun. In the meantime, the ear and nose were dressed accordingly, and I was kept overnight. Not so much for the ear and nose, but because I was still pissing blood from Yuri's shot to my kidney. The doctor wanted to see what color red my urine would be in the morning. The hope was more white Zinfandel than Merlot.

Paul and I were in the same hospital, both victims of a "mugging." He was on a different wing than I was—his wounds far more critical than mine—but I still managed to sneak out later that night and find him. He was out cold, hooked up to an IV that must have been pumping him up with some good stuff, because he didn't even flutter so much as an eyelid when I placed a hand on his forehead.

Someone coughed behind me, and I turned to find a nurse standing in the door. "You really shouldn't be here," she whispered.

"Is he going to be okay?" I whispered back.

She nodded. "You need to let him rest."

I nodded back, gave Paul a final pat, and then walked past the nurse and headed back to my room.

60

Angela was waiting for me on my apartment building steps early that following evening. She was grinning like a kid as I parked and exited, a duffel bag seated next to her.

"Nice teeth," I said with a smirk. Sometime in the last twenty-four hours, she'd gotten a brand new pair of choppers.

She struck a pose, grinning wider and batting her eyes.

"They real?" I asked.

She broke her pose and pulled a *duh* face. "Of course they're not." She flicked her tongue against the slim retainer in her mouth, popping out her front teeth like a tiny pair of dentures.

I smiled. " *Ewww...* "

She grinned and used her tongue again to click her front teeth back home. "I'll only have this for a week. The permanents will be ready by then. They gotta drill 'em in. Should be fun."

I waved a hand at her. "Child's play." I gestured to my nose. "Needs to be *re* -broken." I gestured to my ear. "Needs to be re- *built* ."

"Like Mr. Potato Head," she said with a smirk.

I pointed to her teeth. "Like a meth head."

She shoved me and we went inside.

* * *

We entered my apartment and I instinctively looked towards the floor, expecting Pele to greet me. I felt sad he wasn't there, and then ridiculously happy that I'd be seeing him again. I couldn't wait to get the furry bugger back from my mother's and cuddle the hell out of him.

Angela set her duffel bag on my sofa, turned back to me with a sexy little smile, pulled me in tight, popped up on her toes, went to bring her lips to mine—and ended up with a mouthful of cheek instead.

A split second before her kiss, my mind flashed on the tape, and my head obeyed my mind, turning my profile to her as I gawked at the duffel bag on my sofa. Was it in there?

She slowly pulled her lips from my cheek, her face a splash of dented ego with a hearty base of *what the hell?* Then her eyes tracked mine towards the sofa and her face mellowed into one of comprehension. Eyes back on me, a devilish little smile starting on the corner of her mouth, she said, "You wanna know if I brought it, don't you?"

"Did you?"

"Yes."

"Can I have it?"

"Right now?"

"I'd like to feed it to my garbage disposal."

She went to her duffel bag and retrieved a black DVD case. The devilish little smile now full-grown, she waved the DVD case in front of her in true tantalizing fashion. "Wanna watch it again?" she asked.

"You're kidding, right?"

She continued waving the DVD, continued smiling. "Aren't you just a tiny bit curious? I mean now that it's all over?"

"I've seen it, thank you."

Still waving the DVD: "Going once..."

"Angela."

"Going twice..."

"What the hell is wrong with you?"

She burst out laughing.

I shook my head, laughing a little myself. "You're sick."

She set the DVD on the TV and then cozied up to me again. "Isn't that what you like about me?"

"It does have a certain desirability."

She went in to kiss me then paused. "You're not going to give me your cheek again are you?"

I kissed her. She pulled away and headed towards my bedroom, undressing on the way. She stopped at the doorway, naked, her back to me. Then a glance over her shoulder with carnal fuck-me eyes before disappearing into my bedroom.

I didn't run, but I certainly didn't stroll after her either.

61

Angela dozed on my chest after sex. I couldn't sleep. I was preoccupied with how I was going to tell her about the money. I was also thinking about the DVD out there, sitting atop my TV as though it could have been any number of DVDs I owned. She'd brought it, just as she'd promised, but it was still there—in one piece. I likened it to the survivor of a horrific attack, the aftermath a constant state of insecurity despite knowing their attacker was behind bars. Only when that assailant was in the ground would they *truly* feel safe. I had that DVD behind bars, but wouldn't feel truly safe until it was dead and buried. This I knew. I had to destroy it now.

Aftermath.

My analogy had stirred a deeper, more troublesome realization. Its impact jerked me, and Angela stirred.

"You okay?" she asked.

"Aftermath," I said.

She rolled off my chest and propped herself onto one side. "What do you mean?"

"The aftermath. We discussed it prior, but we haven't discussed it since."

"What's to discuss?"

"Leaving a trail? My blood, my *ear* at the scene? Christ, why am I only realizing this *now* ?"

She raised an eyebrow. "Uh, maybe because you've experienced more trauma in the past twenty-four hours than most would in twenty-four lifetimes? I'm impressed you remember your name."

"No, no—this is bad…"

"Calvin, stop it. The police think it was a robbery gone wrong. They even think it may be drug-related."

I spun on my side and faced her. " *What?* How do you know that?"

"It was on the news."

"When? I never saw anything."

"You were in the hospital."

"Yeah but there was a TV in the room. The news was on. I didn't see anything about a robbery gone bad."

She shrugged. "You were probably stoned on painkillers and missed it." She yawned and curled back into me. "You're in the clear."

"I don't believe it."

She shrugged again and closed her eyes. "You can read about it tomorrow. I'm sure it's somewhere on the internet."

"It can't be that easy, can it?"

Her eyes were still closed, she looked close to drifting. "I told you, they said it was—"

"I know, I just—you see all those crime shows like *CSI* where they talk about DNA and fibers and every other little goddamn thing you'd never consider…"

"That's TV."

Her words and blasé manner helped some, but I just couldn't get my head around the fact that my fucking *ear* could be at a crime scene and somehow not come back to haunt me. Christ, why hadn't I picked the damn thing up and taken it with me? Fine, with Paul dying and all I didn't have time to get down and scrub away my blood and vomit, but at least pick up the goddamn ear!

"I don't see how it can't come back to me," I said.

Angela sighed and opened her eyes. "Give me one— *one* —reason why the police would ever consider you a suspect?"

" *My ear!* "

"Is your DNA on file?"

"How should I know?"

"Have you ever committed a felony?"

"No."

"Then it's not on file. Even if for some inexplicable reason it is, the government is so backlogged, there's a good chance it's not even in the system. You're in the clear, Calvin. Go to sleep."

My mind was racing now. "Okay, forget the police—what if one of Mr. John's people puts the pieces together?"

She groaned. "You know, after what you've accomplished you wouldn't think you were such a pussy." She rolled out of bed, went to my dresser, and snatched the bottle of Oxycontin the doctor had prescribed me for my pain. She then left the room, and I soon heard the water running in the kitchen. She returned with a glass of water and a palm offering two pills.

"Here. It'll help you relax."

I was to only take one pill every four to six hours. "That's gonna knock me the fuck out."

"That's the idea."

Was it any different than drowning my anxieties with booze, which I could *really* go for right now by the way? I took the pills from her and chased them down with the glass of water.

She smiled and got back into bed, curling into me once more and then stroking my chest. "Relax, baby—everything's okay now."

I fell into a deep sleep soon after.

62

Angela was gone when I woke up. I rolled over and checked the clock. Eleven a.m. I certainly had a good excuse for sleeping late, but she probably got restless.

"Angela?"

No reply. No sounds of the shower going, no sounds in the kitchen, no TV.

I sat up. "Angela?" Still nothing.

I made my way out of bed, wincing and groaning every inch of the way. My body felt as if I'd survived a stoning. I threw on an undershirt and a pair of boxers and wandered into my living room.

"Hello?"

The bathroom door was closed. Maybe she was, you know, what we guys call: *in the office* ? I waited a couple of minutes, using the time to check my face in the living room mirror. I certainly hadn't gotten any prettier while I slept. My eyes seemed blacker, and when I peeled off the dressing, my nose bigger, even *more* crooked.

I peeled off the dressing over my ear. At least that didn't look any worse. There was still a fucked-up-looking hole where my left ear used to be of course, but at least it hadn't shed its vanity overnight like my nose seemed to be doing.

I tossed the dressings into the trash and went to the bathroom door again. I'd heard no flush or anything. Maybe she was reading on the John? I know I did. Jesus, I'd never scrutinized a woman's toilet habits so much in my life.

Ah, fuck it; we were past modesty here, weren't we? After all we've been through? I knocked on the bathroom door. "You in there?"

Nothing. I tried the doorknob. It was unlocked. I opened the door and entered my bathroom. No one. I touched my shower floor. It was dry. The sink was dry. My towels were dry. The toilet seat was up. She'd never been, at least not since last night.

I headed into the den. Her duffel bag wasn't on the sofa. Why?

"She just went home," I said aloud. "Wanted to get more of her things." It *needed* to be said aloud. Thoughts race and squirm like a tank of eels. Words are slow and plodding; once spoken they carry a stamp. This needed stamping. "Went home to get more of her things." I nodded in affirmation to my own words. Stamp, stamp, fucking stamp.

I sat on the sofa, took the remote, and pointed it at my TV…and the canvas money belt seated atop my TV.

I leapt from the sofa. There it was, the money belt, coiled on top of my TV like the snake I'd always likened it to. Next to it was the infamous black DVD case. Next to that, an envelope with my name written on the front. I tore open the envelope. A handwritten letter was inside:

Calvin,

I don't know why you felt the need to lie to me about the money. I truly want to believe that you intended on telling me about it eventually, but right now, after all we've been through, my heart is breaking that you would deceive me like this. Perhaps I was right; your trust will never be for sale.

I left you the DVD as part of our agreement. Destroy it and you'll be free.

I doubt you'll hear from me again.

Angela.

I dropped the letter and did a frantic search around the room, as if by some measure of insanity—to which I was more than susceptible by now—I'd been dreaming, that I'd wake, standing where I was standing, newborn and blinking away nothing but fading images of a cruel dream and a sleepwalking episode: there was no money belt on my TV; no letter telling me I was a dick and see ya when I see ya; maybe not even a fucking DVD of me killing anybody.

Oh God yes please do that please it would be so nice please yes please. Or better yet none of it is real I'm crazy it's all been in my head I'm crazy and I've got both my ears and Angela doesn't hate me and I'm just fucking crazy and Angela doesn't hate me and I'm somewhere locked away safe and Angela doesn't hate me…

(*No. Sorry. Nope. No .*)

" *FUCK!* "

I don't remember dressing. I might have left my house naked. I only know I drove to Angela's house, rang her doorbell, banged on the door, and then waited in her driveway until nearly two in the morning. She never answered. No car ever pulled into her driveway either.

In a fit of desperation, I'd smashed one of her windows and climbed in.

No alarm (curiously), but no Angela either. I checked every fucking nook of every fucking room, almost crying as I called her name.

She was gone.

THE BAR

"See? I didn't pull off shit," I say.

The bartender pulls a face. "Are you kidding? You *did* pull it off!"

I laugh and sip my scotch. "Got my friend stabbed. Lost my dream girl. Got my—"

"*Dream girl?*"

I frown at him. "Yeah...?"

"You saying you still trust her?"

"Why wouldn't I? *I'm* the one who fucked up."

He pulls another face. "You sure, man? Maybe you did exactly what she wanted—and now she's done with you."

"What? You mean freeing her from Mr. John?"

"Exactly."

"And the money?"

He shrugs. "Didn't you tell me she was already loaded? Hell, she even left you the money belt. I assume that's where those hundreds you keeping handing me are coming from."

I think on this for a minute.

He interrupts with: "When you think about it, maybe your hiding the money gave her the perfect little out she was looking for."

It's all too much at once. His reasoning is sharp, mine pickled. Try and focus. Money. Go back to that. "Okay then...how did she find the money? Tell me that."

"You hid it in your hamper, man."

"So?"

"You live in a one-bedroom apartment. She drugged the hell out of you—coincidence by the way?—and therefore had ample time to turn over the three, maybe four whopping stones your tiny place has?"

Fuck, he was making sense. Wait, no. "But how would she know I was lying? What if there really *was* no money? What would prompt her to go looking around my place? Assume I was lying?"

The bartender shrugs. "I don't know, man. Maybe she read something in you—knew you were lying about the money from the moment you told her."

I shake my head adamantly. "But she didn't *care* about the money. You just said it yourself."

A sympathetic face. "But she *did* care about the lie. The potential behind it, I mean."

"Why not just leave? Why all the drama with the letter and leaving the money belt on the TV and all? Why not just up and leave as soon as I was asleep?"

More sympathetic face. "Because you would have hated her for it. This way you get to hate yourself."

I drain my scotch. "Good Christ, could she really be that cruel? Knowing me the way she does?"

He fills my glass. The Macallan is half-dead. "So where does that leave you then?"

I sip and say: "What do you mean?"

"I mean what happens now? With you?"

"I guess I don't have to worry about killing anybody anymore."

I laugh.

He frowns.

I frown back at him. "Well what the fuck do you want me to say, man? You want a moral or something?"

He senses my frustration and loosens his frown, takes a step back. "Sure, okay. What's the moral?"

"There *is* no moral. People always want to think everything happens for a reason. Shit just fucking happens. The world doesn't owe you a reason." I drain my scotch. "Morality is for picture books. In life, it's nothing but learned naiveté…keeps us from blowing our brains out if we ever saw people for who they truly are." I hang my head. "The moral is there is no moral…I lost the girl."

"And gained your life."

I look away and start nodding.

"You don't care, do you?" he asks. "About your life…"

I turn back. "I guess I do. I *do* know that I couldn't take another. No way…no way in hell."

"Well that's definitely something."

I give a soft chuckle. "How many people utter such a thing? It's like I'm swearing off the bottle."

He accommodates me with a little chuckle of his own.

I drop my head for a moment. Everything's fuzzy except Angela's face. "I just…I kinda wish I got the girl."

He looks apologetic now. "Hey, man, I could be all wrong you know—my theory about her motives. I mean I wasn't there; I don't know. Maybe it *is* pretty damn straightforward. She stumbled upon the money and felt betrayed. Maybe she just needs some time to cool off."

I nod absently again.

"Seriously, man, let's says my theory is way off. You lied about the money—fine, you're a bad boy. Think about what you gave her. In simplest terms, you saved her life. I think a lie about money—and it wasn't a lie rooted in greed, but in a bid for loyalty—can be forgiven for something as valuable as her life, don't you?"

"Yeah…"

"And you said your friend is going to be okay?"

"Yeah."

He splays his hands. "You took a swan dive into a pool of shit, and while you didn't necessarily come up a rose, at least you came up." He points to my missing ear. "Just missing a few pieces is all."

I laugh and start to wonder if he's a shrink moonlighting as a bartender. He'd certainly have an eclectic pick of subjects to dissect in such a place. Yours truly included.

"Can I call you a cab, man?"

"Sell me a bottle to go first. I don't care what."

"Uh…kind of illegal, bud."

I roll my eyes, thumb ten bills, and then slap them on the bar. A thousand dollars cash. "Still feel law-abiding?"

I'm handed a fresh bottle of Beam.

"Cheers," I say. "Call me that cab."

63

Headache. Shit in my mouth. Nausea.

Hangover.

I open my eyes and the sunlight from my window is like a laser drilling into my brain.

I just wanna sleep.

But it's the kind of hangover that won't let you sleep. The kind that's like a little kid; once it knows you're awake, it's going to make your life hell until you get out of bed and do something about it.

Hair of the dog.

I roll out of bed.

Hair of the dog.

I stumble out of my room.

Hair of the dog.

Why not? Why the fuck not? I'm living in the moment, right?

I stumble towards my kitchen. I'm still buzzed from last night, probably still drunk. That's good; will make my new drunk easier. I'm not sure if I have anything to drink, but I spot a full bottle of Jim Beam sitting on my counter. And then I remember the bar. More importantly, the bar- *tender* . What that guy must think. Well fuck him—living in the moment, me.

I find a glass and fill it with Beam, no ice. The first swig is rough; my stomach hitches. But then the burning, warming sensation follows and it's better. I immediately take another swig. Better than the last—warmer too. I drain the glass and it feels right. A few minutes later, I'm drunk again, and that *definitely* feels right.

I fill the glass halfway again and head over to the sofa. "Living in the moment," I say to no one. I grab the remote. "Not numb anymore. Not watching the movie of myself. Not—"

I stop.

Not watching the movie of myself.

The movie of myself.

It's still there. On my TV. The movie of myself.

Angela's words come back to me like whispers:

"Wanna watch it again? Aren't you just a tiny bit curious? I mean now that it's all over?"

"No." I set my drink down, stand, snatch the DVD case from my TV, open it, pop out the disc, go to snap the bastard in half—and stop.

"Aren't you just a tiny bit curious? I mean now that it's all over?"

"No. I want to watch *Chainsaw* and get drunk."

And yet I put the disc in my DVD player. Hit play and take a seat.

Black screen and then:

An empty room. A solitary chair facing the camera. Angela enters and takes a seat in the chair. She smiles and flicks her fake teeth with her tongue. It's recent.

"Hey, you," she says. "I knew you'd eventually watch it. Do I know my man or what?"

For some reason, I look over my shoulder. The DVD continues.

"I need to show you something, baby," she says. "Please watch carefully."

The scene changes. It is an overhead view from a security camera of what I did to Mr. John at the club. It shows me cutting off his balls. It shows me cutting his throat after. And goddamnit if it doesn't show me smiling as I'm doing it all.

A quick cut and we're back to Angela now. "Questions, yes? Many questions. Let's see, where to begin...well, first off, as you well know, there's no need to edit this gem; you're a cold-blooded killer and I love you for it." She grins. "Oh and I've got plenty of copies if you'd like some. Great as stocking stuffers." She smiles and flicks her fake teeth again. "Okay, you ready for the major newsflash? The men you killed were not Mr. John and his goons. In fact, there never *was* a Mr. John." She leans in close to the camera. "Remember when I told you I had only one major competitor in the industry?" She leans back and splays her arms with a triumphant grin. "Guess who's number one now?"

I can only blink a response.

"Unfortunately, the old saying is true," she says. "You can't make an omelet without breaking a few eggs." She removes her teeth and flashes the gap with a big grin. "Removing my own teeth was *not* pleasant, but it was pretty fucking dramatic, wouldn't you say?"

I nod at the TV.

She puts her teeth back in. "I had a busy night after you left the club, Calvin. It took me and my employees *forever* to clean up the mess you left. Did a number on them, didn't you? You *and* your savior friend. Don't worry, I've got no reason to call on him; I imagine he's fairly clueless to the whole operation, yes? Yeah, I think so. Your moral compass is a curious thing. What to spare and what to take? Fortunately, all I really needed to take was the video footage from the bathrooms. Left my team to take care of the rest; made sure I was able to meet you back at the hotel in time."

"That's why I never saw anything about it on TV," I say.

"That's why you never saw anything about it on TV," she says. "All three of those men might as well have just—" She makes a *poof!* sound "— up and vanished."

I reach for my drink and knock it over. I don't care.

"So in conclusion, my dear Calvin, there never *was* a Mr. John. I'm a very successful, very self-made woman. And you—you wonderful, wonderful man—took care of my only major competition. The future is so very bright, baby. So very bright and so very busy. I'll be in touch soon." She blows me a kiss, grins, and the screen goes black.

I stare silent for a while. Am I numb again? Maybe. It doesn't matter. I get up and walk to my bedroom and grab the bottle of oxys. I head to the kitchen and grab the bottle of Beam. I head back to the den, take out her DVD, toss it across the room, and put in *Chainsaw* . I sit on the sofa, bottle of oxys in one hand, bottle of Beam in the other.

(If you die, she won't care.)

She can't win.

(Think of Paul.)

This bullshit almost got him killed.

(Think of Pele.)

Better he be at my mom's, safe and warm and fed. What kind of security could I hope to offer him?

(She won't care. You're a number to her; that's all.)

I can't let her win.

I swallow a mouthful of oxys and chase it with a deep swig from the bottle of Beam.

The opening monologue by a young John Larroquette is finished. Now flash photos of the corpse The Hitchhiker dug up. I smile. God, I love this film.

I take another handful of pills and chase it with more Beam.

Franklin complaining it's too hot in the van. Marilyn Burns is ridiculously sexy. Blows away any scream queen working today.

I take more pills, more Beam. Things are getting fuzzy. I want to see Leatherface. I want to see what I think is the best scene in cinematic history. I want to see when Leatherface hits Kirk with the sledge, drags him inside, and then slams the steel door shut with the boom to end all booms.

I want...

. . .

. . .

ABOUT THE AUTHOR

A native of the Philadelphia area, Jeff has published multiple works in both fiction and non-fiction. In 2011 he was the recipient of the Red Adept Reviews Indie Award for Horror.

Jeff's debut novel *Bad Games* was a #1 Kindle bestseller that spawned two acclaimed sequels, and now all three books in the terrifying trilogy have been optioned as feature films and are currently being translated for foreign audiences.

His other novels, along with his award-winning short works, have also received international acclaim and are eagerly waiting to give you plenty of sleepless nights.

Free time for Jeff is spent watching horror movies, The Three Stooges, and mixed martial arts. He loves steak and more steak, thinks the original 1974 *Texas Chainsaw Massacre* is the greatest movie ever, wants to pet a lion someday, and hates spiders.

He currently lives in Pennsylvania with his wife Kelly and their cats Sammy and Bear.

Jeff loves to hear from his readers. Please feel free to contact <u>him</u> to discuss anything and everything, and be sure to visit his <u>website</u> to sign up for his FREE newsletter (no spam, not ever) where you will receive updates and sneak peeks on all future works along with the occasional free goodie!

Connect with Jeff on Facebook and Twitter

<u>www.facebook.com/JeffMenapace.writer</u>

<u>http://twitter.com/JeffMenapace</u>

Other Works by Jeff Menapace

Please visit Jeff's Amazon Author Page or his website for a complete list of all available works!

<u>http://www.amazon.com/Jeff-Menapace/e/B004R09M0S</u>

<u>www.jeffmenapace.com</u>

AUTHOR'S NOTE:

Thank you so much for taking the time to read *Numb* . Every single reader is important to me. Whenever I'm asked what my writing goals are, my number one answer, without pause, is to entertain.

I want you to have fun reading what I write. I want to make your heart race. I want you to get paper cuts (or Kindle thumb?) from turning the pages so fast. Again—I want to entertain you.

If I succeeded in doing that, I would be very grateful if you took a few minutes to write a review on Amazon for *Numb* . Reviews can be very helpful, and I absolutely love to read the various insights from satisfied readers.

Thank you so very much, my friends. Until next time…

Jeff Menapace

.